Spunk and Spice

VOLUME 2

B. A. PAUL

Contents

Foreword

"Back in my day" and "It didn't used to be this way" are phrases I'm hearing a lot these days, mostly from folks older than me.

Heck. I'm even starting to say those things. Every few days or so, I hear my mother or grandmother come right out of my mouth.

Things are changing quickly—technology is leaping forward at a breakneck pace. For those born decades before everyone could operate a smartphone before their umbilical cords were cut, it can be a struggle to keep up.

(And don't even get me started on how many television remotes get "un-programmed" in a given week.)

It's a good thing stories are timeless and need no "newfangled doo-dads" to enjoy. Unless you're reading this volume on a screen, then you may need to tinker with a download or adjust your font size.

Otherwise, sit back, unplug from the planet for a bit, and spend some time with the spunky and spicy ones!

Happy reading!

B. A. Paul

So, When I Die

Edward and Phyllis—the perfect lifetime partners through thick and thin. When Phyllis passes, Edward finds the perfect way to honor his dear wife's memory.

Edward draped his tired arm over the back of the well-worn wooden bench. Many evenings he and Phyllis had spent here watching the sun dip below Lake Michigan's rim. Sometimes in blazing summer heat. Sometimes in crisp fall air. Always together. Always with his left arm draped over the bench behind her shoulders. Her nestled into his side.

Connected.

The seat beside him was empty for the first time since before the choppy lake shore grew to the attraction it now is. He and Phyllis courted here with a plaid wool blanket spread on the unkempt sand. A wicker picnic basket held whatever goodies Phyllis had baked.

He shook his head when he remembered the time she'd tricked him. Put the black snake—very much alive and very much angry—in the bottom of the basket. He'd shot up from the blanket, into the lake, and was halfway to Canada before his heart stopped racing. She'd laid back in the sand and guffawed at him. He'd come back to their lunch spot, dripping wet and not too trusting, only after the snake had retreated to the dunes. For the next ten picnics, he'd been the one to pack their basket.

Edward asked why she'd done it. She stretched her legs out, her blond hair falling across her shoulders, and blinked her blue eyes at him. "So, Edward, when I die, you'll have a good story to tell at my funeral." How young they'd been.

And he had the preacher tell that story at her funeral. Most everyone knew it already. Everyone but the preacher, and he hadn't wanted to include such an antic in the eulogy, but Edward insisted.

He and Phyllis had watched, year by year, as the beach grew to a tourist spot. They'd gave up their blanket and picnics when their joints didn't allow for such maneuvers down to the sandy beach and when the beer can and dirty diaper litter kept them on the perimeter.

They settled for long walks down the cement sidewalk toward the fishing pier and lighthouse. Then they'd laid claim to the bench. Watching the walkers and joggers and lovers and haters. Children dragging mothers to the water's rippling edge. Mothers dragging children, sand caked to their bare legs and feet, back to the walkway. Back to the parking lot.

Phyllis and Edward had been actors in that scene more than once with their own children. Even now, his own children and his children's children waited in the parking lot, or maybe they were skipping in the opposite direction of the bench. He didn't know. But he was glad they'd given him some moments alone—well, as alone as one could be on a public beach—before Phyllis's final send-off party.

A drone buzzed overhead. Edward leaned forward from his seat a bit to see if he could spot the police officer manning the flying machine, but the man—or lady cop—was too far down the beach. He remembered when the drones came. At first he thought it was a kite or a remote-control airplane some teenager had spent his allowance on. Over the years, he and his wife had watched more than one meltdown over unintended water landings of such not-so-waterproof craft. Tears and squawks and boohoos over the gadgets Lake Michigan swallowed up.

But the drones were different. Crime increased. Police force numbers were down. So they employed eyes to the sky and, if a ruckus or problem arose, a cop or two on four-wheelers would come flying down the beach. Phyllis had spotted the drones first and figured out what was happening. "It's so if someone's down here mooning the boardwalk, the police can respond right quick to catch it first-hand." She'd grinned at him. Eyes still as blue as when they dated. "So keep your pants on, old man."

And they'd seen plenty of full moons on the boardwalk.

The drone flew past Edward's bench and hovered over the fishing pier. His hearing was going, but he could tell by the small groups' collective body language that things were heating up. Waving arms. Hands on hips. Stomping off when someone pointed at the aerial surveillance. The group dispersed. No cops came rushing down the beach. Too bad.

Edward and Phyllis always liked waiting for those white and black four wheelers.

Edward leaned back on the bench and stretched his legs out in front of him. His dark trousers soaked up the sun's rays. He'd have been more comfortable in his golf shorts, but they'd come straight from the funeral home. The drone floated and bobbed back in the opposite direction. Edward waved at it and draped his arm back over the side, smiling.

Phyllis. That day with the drone. He'd never know how long the idea had played in her head. How long she'd planned the antic or if it just…happened.

After a similar instance where the drone managed to break up a potentially volatile situation, on its way back, Phyllis decided to follow it. Waving. Half jogging, half running.

Which brought a four-wheeler, because Edward was trying to get her to stop. And the eyes in the sky thought something was wrong with the old couple. Or that Edward was after her. When the young, straight-outta-training lad came rushing to her aid, she assured the man that Edward was harmless, a pussy cat really. She'd batted those crystal blue eyes at him and said she wanted to know if the cop and his buddies were really watching. And to thank him for his service. "And, by the way, kind officer, could I have a ride?"

And without waiting for a reply, she'd flung one leg over the back of the four-wheeler, situated herself on the seat behind the young man, wrapped one arm around him, pointed straight ahead with the other, and shouted "Onward!" The boy turned all kinds of red, as did Edward, and the officer took off with Phyllis whooping and laughing up and down the beach.

Carl, his name was. He was at the funeral today. And Phyllis had gotten him to give her more than one ride on the four-wheelers, but only after she'd promised not to wave down the drone unless something was wrong. Carl promised to find her if he was on duty. He'd offered Edward rides, but Edward allowed Phyllis all the glory. Enjoying her enjoying herself.

When their son asked her what she was thinking, she replied, "So when I die, you'll have a good story to tell at my funeral."

Carl, more man than boy from that first night on the beach, told this one. With a stern warning to the funeral-goers not to wave down drones—lest the spunky gene run in the family.

Edward could see his family making their way toward him. Good-looking group, even if he was biased. They bumped and amoeba-d their way along the sidewalk, sometimes stopping to let the kids meander off the walkway onto the sand. The beach wasn't all that crowded this evening, for which he was glad. Phyllis liked to people watch, but Edward wanted some privacy tonight. His son had Phyllis's ashes tucked under his arm.

It'd been a long day.

It'll be a long few months, adjusting to the empty space on the bench.

The empty seat at the dining room table for two in their tiny beach house three streets up from the dunes.

The empty spot in the bed next to him.

He watched as his daughter swatted the two-year-old's rear. The boy had tried to taste the sand. Edward's son and his wife had their hands full with pre-teenagers. Tweens they call them now. Everything had a label. Phyllis didn't like that. Political correctness was never her strong suit. Phyllis pretty much said what was on her mind.

"Let the words fall where they fall. Call a duck a duck, an idiot an idiot."

He guessed by the pace the group was walking that he had about five more minutes. Maybe ten if the kids kept getting distracted.

That was another game the couple had played. How long do you think that person/group/child/cop will take to get from the lamppost at the corner of the parking lot all the way to the worn wooden bench? They'd gotten pretty good at it. Even played around on their Jitterbug phone with the timer and could nail down most passerby's rates to ten-second ranges.

The toddlers always made things interesting, though. "The wild-cards of life!" Phyllis would say.

The breeze blew off the water, sending a shiver of cold over Edward's bones despite the funeral suit's layers. Edward felt for the fat, black permanent marker in his inside suit pocket. It was still there. He'd planned on passing it on to his son. Just before, but not too soon.

Further down the beach, a group of young men were whooping and goofing off. One guy, young and dumb, passed off his canned beverage to one of the buddies and took off ripping through the water, cartwheeling and failing miserably. The group laughed and journeyed on with their drenched, foolish friend.

Fitting. Edward smiled again. Phyllis's other favorite thing to do after their bodies had slowed down was to spot the "hold this" moments. Where an idiot got an idea and the idiot's buddies gave audience and helped by holding the beer can, or fishing pole, or whatever.

She and Edward would laugh and then retell their own—mostly her—"hold this" moments.

The family was half the distance to the bench they'd been a minute ago. The toddler, wild hair blowing in all directions, sticking to his face, had fallen in line and held on to mommy's hand. He remembered silhouettes of Phyllis holding their children's hands through the years. Walking this beach after a long day. Or early summer mornings. "To wear the little rascals out so you and I can have some fun later, Ed." Then she'd wink. With those Caribbean, crystal blue eyes.

Carl was coming up the beach, too, small shovels tucked alongside him on the four-wheeler. Edward stood to stretch. It was about time to put Phyllis to rest. Though she'd not like that phrase. She'd want to be out bopping and frolicking and getting into mischief. But she'd agreed to this place. To keep Edward company for as long as he could make it to the boardwalk. His old legs, happy to accompany Phyllis on what-ever grand adventures she'd dreamed up were stoving up. It was today or never. He felt for the marker again and twisted his wedding band nervously.

"Ready, Dad?" His daughter laid her head on his shoulder and rubbed his back. She looked like her mom. Blond. Blue-eyed. Phyllis lives on. He returned the gentle half-hug and focused down on his wedding band again.

Phyllis had twirled it that last day at the beach house. There in the bathroom. The day she'd decided to go into the hospital for pain control. "I need your help, Edward." She'd stood in front of the mirror and looked at her reflection next to his. She reached up and felt his cheek. He bent down and kissed her gray hair. Still gorgeous. Her eyes still blue, though dulling, more Lake Michigan than Caribbean.

"Anything."

She twisted his wedding band. "You're not gonna like it."

He'd smiled at her. "That's what you've said before all of our grandest memories."

She handed him a black permanent marker and undid the top couple of buttons of her nightgown. "I want you to write what I tell you. Right here." She ran her finger along the underside of her collar bone. Just above her heart. Her hand trembled. Phyllis hated hospitals. She'd wanted to pass at home, but things escalated quickly. No time for hospice set-up. No time for planning. Just diagnosis and pain.

"I'm confused—"

She brought his hand holding the uncapped marker to her skin. "I'm scared, Ed. I don't want to linger. I want to be free. So, I want you to write right here." She pointed again. He nodded.

"Write: So, when I die, let me be," her voice shook. "This way, they'll see. And they won't try…"

Edward's hand paused. She'd turned to look at him straight in the face. Took his scruffy cheeks in her hands. "Please." She twirled his wedding band on his left hand as he wrote with his right. The Do Not Resuscitate order, Phyllis style, under her collar bone.

At the hospital, the nurses fell in love with Phyllis. His wife's personality oozed out wherever she went, despite her pain. One gal, Serena, senior nurse, said "Now, I've seen it all."

She'd taken great care of Phyllis in those last days. And she'd been at the funeral, too. And Serena had helped Edward with his own permanent marker request—after some protesting, of course, and assurances that Edward wasn't trying anything, well, final.

"Quite the opposite, Serena. Quite the opposite. I'm taking a page from Phyllis's book on life." He'd winked at the old nurse and she'd happily complied with his request.

Now his family—what he and Phyllis had spent years creating and nurturing—arrived at the bench. Carl stood with shovels ready. And the younger men got to work as Edward cradled his wife in his hands for the last time. The funeral director had shown him urns of all sorts. He found the loudest, brightest one. A lime green one with purple streaks. Loud and proud. Like his beloved.

He patted the top of the box and laid it gently in the sandy earth.

He stood back as Carl led the efforts to wrap Phyllis in her favorite beachy earth. Near her favorite bench.

As Edward watched, he started unbuttoning, his hands shaking. Sweating. He thought about backing out, but he was old enough to get away with such antics. Maybe they'd blame it on massive grief and loss. But it was now or never for Edward's "hold this" moment.

He could taste the sweaty salt on his lips as he fiddled with the shirt buttons. Then his trouser buttons. Then his zipper. A smile broke over his wrinkled face. No one was watching him. They were all watching her.

Once all the things that bound him into the funeral suit were loosened, he retrieved the permanent marker. He slipped out of his shoes. Still no one was watching him. Not even the little ones looked back toward the water.

Off came the socks.

Edward dropped the suit jacket to the bench's back rest. He pulled his son aside and handed him the fat pen.

"Here, Son. Hold my marker."

Before the young man could respond, Edward ripped off the dress shirt, stepped out of the suit pants and took off running toward Carl's four-wheeler wearing nothing but blue and white polka-dotted boxers and a block-lettered message scrolled across his back: SO WHEN I DIE...

He jumped onto the ATV, started the engine—thankful Carl had left the key in the ignition—and took himself on his first joy ride.

Well, that's not accurate.

Life with Phyllis was a complete and utter joy ride. Every day.

What a rush! As he sped down the beach, sand kicking up against his bare back and legs, his family shouted warnings over the engine's rev and the tweens whooped and cheered. He braked hard and turned back toward them for another pulse-pounding pass.

So they'd get this moment good and imbedded in their minds.

So when he died, this would be the first of many good stories to tell at his funeral.

Daisy Do

Marla was forever upgrading to the best and the greatest, spending money she and Eddie didn't have—even from beyond the Great Divide...

Eddie Major wiped a stray tear from his sun-leathered cheek and straightened his posture, the shoulder pads inside his Sunday-best navy-blue suit falling into their proper places, and rightly so after years of use. Like a hug from an old friend. He tried to straighten his posture—but not too much. He coaxed another stray tear or two through the ductwork.

Folks were watching, after all. From all corners of the funeral parlor —standing in the corners by the audacious bouquets of carnations and tiger lilies, sitting in the far rows of fading burgundy chairs. From the snack table. From the vestibule where they huddled in twos and threes, pretending to admire the autumn swirl of colors from the oaks lining the sidewalk outside.

Folks expected him to lose his collective good sense and fall to his knees right in front of the casket onto the paisley carpet. But he wasn't going to do that. For one, he was rather fond of the outcome of his double knee replacement and wouldn't risk the impact. For two, he truly could only muster a stray tear every now and then, and maintaining the downcast affect was taking what little emotional energy he had left.

All this touchy-feely pretense only because folks were watching.

Whispers around the tiny three-room funeral parlor were that Eddie would lose it when he got home to his empty house. Without Marla to direct him in all things daily living, what would he do? The Majors' daughters were grown, hitched, and gone—sure to flee to their own homes three states away as soon as Marla's grave descended, and the condolence bouquets of lilies and daisies lay scattered on top of the fresh dirt heap in Arlett Cemetery.

Yes. In just a few short hours, so went the whispers, when husband and wife of forty years, two months and five days were separated by eight feet of earth, Eddie Major would officially be Arlett's newest widower, destined to don bib overalls and take his breakfasts of greasy eggs and brick-hard toast with the other widowed geezers at Gina's Diner. Feast on microwaved meatloaf for his dinners. Wear a butt-shaped hole in the fabric of his hunter green recliner in between those meals as he drinks three-day old coffee and soaks up reruns of war shows on the History Channel.

Or so the whispers said.

The folks thought Eddie couldn't hear their muffled gossip. At sixty-three, and though he had double knee replacement and a hernia repair, to his knowledge, those procedures did not affect his hearing.

If anything had ever damaged his auditory function, it would've been Marla's nagging.

Which is precisely why, Eddie thought, that his girls fled three states away. Marla could nag and opinionate even the strongest of souls to do her will… and the girls, as attentive as they could be from a distance, had more than enough of their mother.

He understood. After long days in the classroom, would find himself sitting outside in the sun or wind or snow for hours upon hours to avoid Marla's nagging inside the house. He'd mow the grass when it didn't need to be mowed. Pull weeds—both real and imaginary. Their driveway was the most impeccable drive on their road. Not a stone out of place. Anything for a little peace and quiet.

The talk of the town, actually.

And the town never stops talking…

Earlier, when the reception line had slowed and Eddie dared to step away from the head of the casket to grab a handful of grapes from the snack table, he'd overheard a few of those whispers between the town vet and some of the overly chatty members of Marla's quilting bee brigade.

He specifically made out "daisies" and "gonna be so mad."

"Mad about what, Luke?" That question came out a little too forceful, so Eddie popped several grapes into his mouth and pretended to dab his eyes with a napkin. Perhaps the dabbing will redden them up or prompt more free-flowing tears.

He was a man overcome with grief, after all, folks had to expect he'd be all over the place with his tone and demeanor.

"Oh, Eddie. I didn't see you there." Luke, the middle-aged veterinarian that Marla couldn't speak highly enough of, shifted his weight and stammered on. "How's the cat? Doing okay? Everything okay at home? I know how much Marla just adored that precious baby. If you need anything, anything at all. Sometimes pets grieve too. And how close they were... If Dais—"

"Cat's fine, Luke. Getting fatter by the day." Over Eddie's dead body was he going to spend another dime outside of litter and basic food for that feline. Neither daughter wanted to pack the feline up and house it elsewhere. Not that he could blame them. That cat had a disposition that only Marla could match. Aloof. Cold. Ungrateful...

He certainly would be cutting back on the creature's portion of tuna that belongs on Eddie's rye bread and not scraped directly into the fish-shaped food bowl on the floor.

When things settle after the funeral, he'll call Luke and see if he could rehome Marla's "precious baby." The cat was fixed and vetted thoroughly. His checkbook proved it. Luke could've sent his two kids and three nephews to a few weeks of college given what Marla paid for that stray to be "healthed up" as she put it.

Since a stranger wouldn't make the connection between Marla's moods and the cat's demeanor, it should be easy to find it another. Eddie did, after all, have diners to visit and greasy eggs to down on a daily basis. No time for a pet with his struggling widower life.

An arm encircled his shoulders and gently tugged him back to the front of the room. Back to her.

"You okay, there, Eddie?" Hank from Hank & Sons Construction had been hanging close to the front of the room all morning. The man who called himself Eddie's friend likely felt obligated to be so attentive. Especially since Marla had upgraded a simple window repair job after a tree branch cracked a single pane to an entire house full of super-dee-duper energy efficient windows, including a breakfast nook bump-out with floor-to-ceiling glass.

"Easier to clean and lets in more natural light, Eddie. The curtains were blowing when the old windows were shut! These curtains don't blow any longer." She fluffed the white lacy fabric, tucking the hems so they hung perfectly at their living room window. "You'll thank me when I'm gone."

Well, she's gone, and neither his wallet – nor his mouth – ever thanked Marla for going behind his back and singlehandedly paying for Hank's daughter's first semester of community college with that sneaky move.

Eddie cleared his throat. "Fine as can be, Hank. Thanks for being here."

"No problem, buddy. You call me anytime, now. Anytime." He gave another long, firm squeeze to Eddie's shoulders and walked back to whisper something to Vicki along the lines of "not so great."

See. Nothing much wrong with his hearing.

Vicki was the travel agent/notary public/bank teller extraordinaire who "upgraded" their simple cabin on their twentieth wedding anniversary cruise to the deluxe suite with the balcony. She tilted her head and sent Eddie a pitiful sympathy nod.

He'd scrimped and saved for a simple vacation cruise that year. And with his English teacher salary, it took a lot of scrimping and saving. Marla, ever so set on having the best of the best, just didn't leave it be. When they boarded the ship, Eddie told the bellman he must've escorted the couple to the wrong room. "Oh, no, Mr. Major, this is your room. Only the best for our elite passengers."

Marla had nudged him hard in the ribs. Eddie had stared in shock at the plush accommodations. She'd flipped that braid over her shoulder and smirked proudly. "We only have one twentieth wedding anniversary. You'll thank me when I'm gone." He still remembers shoving his fists into his pockets to keep from shoving her right off the balcony into the bay.

And there she lay. Still gone. Still in that casket. And Eddie no closer to thanking her for such an expenditure.

And that casket.

That casket. Her latest and final upgrade.

Mr. Stone of Arlett Funeral Home was not one bit pushy with the older couple as they had prearranged their funeral plans a decade ago. The Majors hadn't wanted their two girls to have to bear the financial burden or the decision-making under the grief of the loss of a parent. The couple was being frugal and responsible. Mr. Stone gave them space to look at the caskets and vaults and laid out all the service and burial options.

Mr. Stone was not one bit pushy.

But when Eddie remembered back, Marla had flipped that braid from one shoulder to the other and smiled and smiled…Mr. Stone wasn't pushy because he knew — he *knew*, as did the whole town — when the time came, Marla would upgrade.

Marla must've known the end was near for her. Mr. Stone must've known, too, because a phone call and a couple of grand later, Marla had upgraded her final resting place. Gone was the frugal and simple.

Ushered in was this, this… Rolls-Royce of caskets. And the bank statement didn't reflect the upcharge until Marla had already passed and it was too late and too complicated to change anything. "Only the best for your wife, Mr. Major," Mr. Stone had offered in the most comforting of tones.

He turned toward the casket as the minister touched his elbow. "It's time, Eddie."

Time for one last glimpse of her form. The final goodbye. Eddie gazed on his wife's ashen face, her whiter-by-the-year braid arranged over her shoulder. It was his Marla, but at the same time, it wasn't. The mortician did her best, but dead is dead. If Eddie stared long enough, he could almost see that classic smirk form at the left corner of her mouth. With his keen hearing, he could swear he heard her say, "You'll thank me, Eddie. Soon. You'll thank me."

He inhaled and shuddered a bit.

Eddie rested his hand on the edge of the casket. All eyes were on him. So he carefully, slowly moved his leathered hand to cover her folded ones. Coldness greeted him. He wasn't surprised. Coldness radiated from Marla even before she was laid out in her upgraded casket adorned with yellow embroidered daisies.

Daisies.

His shoulders slumped. The crowd would believe it an appropriate reaction to a last caress.

But the decoration on the casket insert, the view Marla would forever have behind her closed lids, was daisies.

Not a single daisy.

Plural.

Many, many daisies.

Even in her death, she's still sticking it to him.

A rush of heat rose from Eddie's gut and turned his face red. His hands began to shake, and he could feel a bead of sweat form on his upper lip.

So right there.

Right there in the funeral parlor in his Sunday-best suit and with his strong new kneecaps. Right there in front of Luke, Mr. Stone, Hank and his sons and well-educated daughter. Right there in front of the travel agent and the quilting bee ladies and the minister.

Right there.

He leaned down close to Marla's ear.

And shouted loud enough for Marla to hear him from beyond the veil:

"Her name is Daisy, you nag of a wife!"

And then everything went black.

A rush of cool air wafted over Eddie's frame. Someone had removed his Sunday best jacket and laid it across his midsection. He shirt sleeve was rolled up. Squeezing and pinching brought him around a bit further. He blinked a few times to clear the blur. The hum of an engine told him the bright lights were from the interior of an ambulance and not the ceiling of an Arlett Memorial ER room.

To his right a young woman fiddled with an IV and blood pressure cuff. To his left, the ever faithful Mr. Stone patted his shoulder and told him everything would be okay. That folks were waiting patiently, and prayers were being prayed, and well wishes were being wished, and leftovers were being packed up from the snack table to be taken to his home later—so he could have sustenance to get through the day. And that he should really mind his fluid intake under times of great grief and loss. "One can get dehydrated so easily. And just drop. Drop like a fly on a hot August day, even in the cool of fall."

The last few moments with Marla's corpse came back to him. The anger. The rage. Frustration.

But Eddie certainly felt no grief.

The EMT asked him about his medications. He rattled off the few over the counter things he took. And the name of his blood pressure medicine. A pill he likely wouldn't need to swallow anymore now that Marla's nagging has stopped. But he kept this plan to himself lest the EMT and Mr. Stone scold him on how to live his life.

He'd had quite enough of that with Marla.

He closed his eyes and let his two commrades go about their duties, the one for his body, the other for his emotions. He recalled the embroidery all around his wife. The upgrade that he'd not approved of.

"You'll thank me when I'm gone..."

A machine beeped over his head. "Mr. Major, your pressure's rising. Try to remain still and think of calm, things."

Yeah, right. Calm. Not while visions of dainty white flowers and bold yellow centers filled his mind.

The logical part of Eddie's brain, the reasonable part that saw him through a successful career as an English teacher, knew the fight over Daisy single and Daisies plural was not rational. But it was a tiff that was always there. He remembered back to that very first conversation when the cat was just a kitten, less than a year old.

"Daisies is plural. I should know. I was an English teacher for—"

"For your whole life. I know. I like the name. I like the flowers. That's her name. You won on the gender. I win on the name."

"I didn't *win* on the gender, Marla. The cat's got no balls. He's not a he. He's a she. I paid for a spay. Not a neuter. I should know, I—"

"You've kept the checkbook balanced to the penny since the day we were married." She flipped her long gray braid over her shoulder, smirking. And under her breath, though loud enough for his still-good ears to hear, "And I've done all the rest."

Marla was banging around at the sink, fussing with dishes that didn't need fussing with just to make a point. It wasn't Eddie's fault the stray she picked out at the shelter was improperly sexed. He'd given in to her nagging to get a pet. A cat at that. And since they'd raised the two girls, Marla wanted to adopt a boy cat. How can you go wrong when the twenty-something volunteer at the shelter tags the orange baby feline as male? Marla got ticked off that the cat wasn't a he after all.

Giblets the Magnificent turned out to have no giblets at all.

"Well, you didn't have a problem with *Giblets* when we thought he was a boy. And Giblets is plural."

"Giblets makes sense. Daisies doesn't even make sense. I'm not calling her Daisies. I'm calling her Daisy."

"Daisies." The braid flipped to the other shoulder.

"Daisy will do."

"Daisies."

Eddie fiddled with the sleeve of his suit coat. He lifted it up to the light. The lint roll job from this morning missed a couple of stray orange hairs. That cat should've been Giblets. It's an eighty-twenty chance an orange cat should've been a boy. Giblets would've solved a lot of fussing…

On and on it went, for years. Plural. Singular. Different iterations of the same fight. Throw in Marla's propensity for upgrades and spending Eddie's carefully saved retirement funds, and sometimes the fights over the cat's name served as surrogate arguments for other, more heated issues.

Through it all, Daisy remained aloof, not caring in the least what her name might be. Sunning herself in a window. Licking herself on the kitchen counter. Batting lazily at one of the plush catnip toys or fancy feather teasers Marla dropped hundreds of dollars on a year. The living room floor looked as if they owned a shelter full of strays instead of just the one spoiled rotten one.

Spoiled beyond belief.

Eating a good portion of Eddie's tuna from that stupid fish-shaped bowl…

"You're going to confuse her if I call her Daisies and you call her Daisy."

"She can't be confused. The S is hardly noticeable, Marla."

"Well, *I* know it's there. It's plural. Giblets to Daisies."

"This is one cat. One cat. One Daisy."

"She'll get all of your tuna tomorrow!"

"As a matter of fact, I'm calling her Daisy Do. I like the alliteration. I am an English teacher after all…"

"Don't you dare—"

"Tsk, tsk, come here, Daisy Do!"

The argument was such a fussy mess that at all future vet visits, the staff and Dr. Luke referred to the cat as Marla's Precious Baby lest the couple get started in the waiting room and set everyone – humans and animals—on edge.

Mr. Stone helped the EMT set Eddie upright in the ambulance, eventually maneuvering him to the edge of the bumper into the fresh air. The EMT removed the IV, but left the blood pressure cuff. "Mr. Major, it's totally understandable if you want to delay the burial. We could place Marla—"

Eddie heard dollar signs. Another upgrade in the bill for "storing" his dead wife for another day or two.

"No, no. I'll be fine. I just want this over with!" he snapped, then remembered himself and softened. "Sorry. I really want to put my wife to rest and go home."

"Understood."

The EMT insisted he wait another fifteen minutes to ensure he wasn't at risk of stroke. The friends and neighbors had moved outside, hugging jackets and coats around their bodies to shield against the breeze that had picked up. Browns and reds and yellows swirled through the air and scuttled across the pavement of the parking lot. Eddie watched them huddle in small groups. Still gossiping. Likely replaying his outburst at the casket. His backside hurt. He supposed when he blacked out he landed backward—good thing. He'd not wanted to go down on those good knees.

From his perch on the edge of the ambulance, while the EMT fiddled with the cuff and helped him on with his suit jacket, he watched as Hank and Luke and Hank's sons carry his wife's Rolls Royce down the side ramp of the funeral parlor and slide it into the back of the hearse.

He managed a thank you to the EMT. Mr. Stone helped him the rest of the way to his feet.

Time to get this over with. Daisy Do would need her tuna soon, anyway.

∼

Though the events at the graveside had transpired without fanfare or further outbursts, Hank insisted he drive Eddie home, given the heavy weight of sorrow Eddie bore. He'd arranged for Mr. Stone to come behind them in Eddie's sedan – upgraded, of course, to the upper trim level.

As always, the driveway was impeccable. Only yesterday Eddie had blown the fallen leaves down to the curb. Only a few dared to dot the asphalt. "You sure you'll be okay here alone? I can stick around."

"No thanks, Hank. I'm good now. All hydrated up and everything." Eddie patted his arm where the Coban wrap the EMT had applied over the IV site was strangling the circulation down to his fingers. He slid out of Hank's truck. Mr. Stone parked the sedan, a little crooked, but Eddie would fix that later.

"Don't forget this!" Mr. Stone handed Eddie the container of leftovers from the snack table. Eddie planned on a nice, fat tuna on rye, but he said thanks anyway and made his goodbyes without inviting the men in.

The Major's home of over three decades stood strong. Eddie spent meticulous hours and days on its exterior while Marla spent major dough on the inside. He stood in his drive for a few seconds, examining the structure. For the first time in over three decades, he felt he could finally breathe. Bathe in the blessed, blessed silence. No nagging. No begging. No fits and fusses and fights.

No more singular or plural.

Inside, Eddie slipped out of his suit jacket, rolled up his sleeve and removed the adhesive wrap. He rubbed the crook of his arm where the IV had replenished him enough to get through the day's ordeal. He was glad to be away from the pitiful stares and fretful whispers of what his fate might be now that he's on his own. Curse his wickedly good hearing.

He poured himself a glass of water from the sink and allowed his gaze to zone out the window. No one interrupting.

No one suggesting the next project or expenditure.

But a few sips in, he heard something. Then it was gone. Thought he heard something again. High pitched squeaks.

Probably Daisy fussing about, trying to get his attention because it was well past her tuna time.

He grabbed her fish dish from the floor and popped open a can of tuna. He doled out just a tiny bit—Marla would roll over in her upgraded casket—and put it back on the floor. "Daisy Do. Tsk, tsk. Here kitty…"

The noise again, a little louder but no closer. That cat never misses an opportunity to visit the fish dish…

He rounded the corner into the living room. The squeaking intensified. Multiple squeaks. And a lower, longer meow.

The high-pitched squeaks were coming from Daisy Do's Corner Cottage (a top-of-the-line cat retreat hotel Marla found online and made Eddie assemble post haste the day it arrived). The cardboard construction took up most of one wall, and was nearly as tall as Eddie. Big enough for a colony of cats, very much overkill for one Daisy. Single.

He peeked inside one of the windows. Then another, then another, allowing his ears to lead him to the source.

He got down on both new knees, sinking into the plush, top-of-the-line carpet Marla insisted on installing last year. "You'll thank me one day. No more cold, hard wood for our old bones."

There. On the first floor, huddled back in the darkest corner of the cottage, Daisy Do looked up at him and released a long, low howl. And at her side, a ball of wet, squirming squeakers.

"Daisy Do, what did you do?"

That black-out sensation from earlier threatened the corners of his vision. He closed his eyes and breathed deeply, willing blood pressure and stroke-level panic to subside to a dull roar.

"Daisy! What did *Marla* do?" The cat laid her head down as the bundle of babies found their way to food. Eddie got off his knees and sat cross-legged in front of the cottage, peering into the structure.

The fight in the kitchen that night came back to him. *"You've kept the checkbook balanced to the penny since the day we were married."* The flip of the braid. The smirk. Her signature combo move when she'd one-upped him on a decision.

He should've known when the animal didn't come home from the clinic the day after surgery. She likely only boarded the cat for the same amount of money that the spay would've cost. And the performance. His Marla should've been on Broadway! The way she ooed and gooed over Daisy when she returned from her "surgical ordeal."

"Oh, Daisies, look how fast your belly hair grew back!"

"Oh, Daisies, how well you're recovering from your boo boos!"

"Oh, Daisies, here's some extra tuna. The protein will help mommy's precious baby heal up so quick and strong!"

And she'd flip that braid and smirk at the cat. Then smirk at Eddie.

Eddie never paid much attention to Daisy back then, content to let Marla dote and take the attention away from him for even the slightest amount of time. He'd never noticed the lack of a surgical scar—didn't even think to look or pet the cat's stomach.

He fished his phone out of his pocket and tapped on the flashlight. Careful not to blind Daisy, he carefully examined the momma and babies without touching. He didn't see any signs of distress. All the babies were breathing and eating. Daisy's breathing was more regular than Eddie's.

Daisy had… daisies. Eddie counted four—no five—five little bitty orange balls.

Five. Plural.

Eddie flipped off the light. He couldn't think back of a time when Daisy got out of the house—or even if there was a time when Marla took her out of the house. But it happened. The timing had to be around the time Marla's diagnosis came in.

Eddie struggled to stand—but not because of his knees, mind you. He was tired from the day.

Tired from the people. Wanting peace and quiet from the whole ordeal. Tuna on rye and the evening news in his well-worn recliner. Like a hug from an old friend.

And now this. He supposed Daisy was hungry after *her* ordeal today. He called Luke and left a message—it was after hours, after all. Or the man was avoiding his calls because he knew this was coming and was in on it with Marla. The whole town was in on Marla's obsession with upgrades.

In the kitchen, Eddie retrieved the fish dish and topped it off with the entire can of tuna. He'd make do with grapes and cheese from the funeral's snack table and put a plate of hodge podge leftovers together for himself.

He brought the fish dish to the cozy cottage and, in true waiter style, offered it to her on bended knee. Daisy rose slowly, leaving a pile of squirming bitty ones nosing into the air, wondering where their personal heating pad went to.

She started lapping up the tuna, purring at the same time. Always looking back at the babies.

Eddie retired to his recliner to munch on the leftovers and wait for Luke to call back. A photo of Marla and Eddie on that cruise sat on the side table next to his chair. She'd paid extra for that, of course. The crystal blue waters behind them. Marla's braid hadn't turned gray yet. Her smile—not a smirk, a smile—lit the photo up. It had been a nice trip.

He put his plate down. Suddenly not hungry.

He stared past the lacy curtains out to the driveway where he'd escaped so many times. A gust of wind blew more leaves across the blacktop. The curtains, though, remained completely still, the room perfectly insulated from any outside drafts thanks to the quality windows. The evening sun glinted off the sedan in the drive, the chrome trim gleaming in the rays. It's a quality vehicle. Sure to last Eddie quite a long time.

Tears in his eyes, he stood and went to the cottage where Daisy had finished her tuna and was attending to her babies. He knelt once again on the plush carpet, the upgraded pad underneath cushioning his new kneecaps.

And then it hit him. How truly grateful he was for all she did, and now she's gone. His dear, wild, defiant Marla is gone, forever surrounded by embroidered little daisies.

Tears fell freely. No need to hide them. He sat back cross-legged and let them come. Daisy Do emerged from the cottage, a baby dangling from her mouth. She dropped the kid into Eddie's lap. Made four more trips, bringing each of her children to him, her tail held high, her head even higher. Showing off.

Smirking, even, just a little.

If the cat had a braid, she'd have flipped it over her shoulder.

"Well, Daisy Do, I guess it's me and you and your brood from here on." He patted the cottage wall. "There's room for all, thanks to Marla." Daisy curled beside him, peeking every now and then into his lap at her five little upgrades.

Thanks to Marla.

Hiram Lloyd's Handshake Revival

Never take for granted the power of human connection…

I t took nearly a generation after the Powers That Be eradicated nearly all disease and declared their blessed social distancing to be a thing of God Almighty for Hiram Lloyd to lose all reason. He was just fifty back then.

Old by some standards.

Young by others.

And now, at 85, Hiram was as ancient as they come. One of the lucky ones. One to escape the virus, the two mutations that came after, and be counted worthy—given his agricultural background and extensive knowledge of hybrid seeds—to be allotted a ventilator when the third mutation finally took hold in his bottom lung lobes and threatened to bury him as deep as the seeds in his corn field.

Well, who was he kidding? There was no more room to *bury* anyone.

He'd have been incinerated and Gabe would've had to decided what to do with poor Granddad Hiram's ashes.

Hiram slid from the seat of the tractor and rubbed the arthritis knots in his hands and allowed his neck and knees ample time for their ever-familiar popping. On the clear-blue sky days such as this, he afforded himself the luxury of powering up the John Deere—more rust than green—and chugging it down the beaten county road—more pothole than asphalt—two miles to the country church—more lean-to than place of worship.

The gravel in the lot had long since washed away, leaving behind rutted mud in some places. Weeds and yard-worthy green lush thrived where Pastor Dickey used to park. Hiram's occasional trips here to walk him down memory lane and pay respects did nothing to keep the spaces beaten down enough to even call it a parking lot.

But today wasn't a memory-lane kind of day. Yes, he wanted another ride on his tractor, dear friend it had been to him. Yes, he wanted to come early to pay respects. Yes, he wanted to see the morning glories—likely for the last morning. Morning glories for his sweet Glory, long ago scattered here after the first virus tidal wave ripped her from him.

And to remember their only son. Also here, resting with his mother in dusty solitude. Mutation two got hold of Will, and Will's wife, sweet thing she was, fell while caring for her own aging ones.

That left Hiram to raise Gabe.

That left lots of folks raising other people's children, family or not.

But today, Hiram decided long ago, that today Gabe would help him one-up those Powers That Be and teach the young ones a thing or two about country living. Country hospitality.

If only a very small aspect of it.

Starting with his very own grandson.

Who, at the ripe old age of thirty has never shaken another human being's hand. Not skin-to-skin, at least.

Hiram shook his head at the ridiculousness of it all as he stood in the middle of the lot and took in the fields. Nothing but rolling fields planted with the latest tech bots nestled against the church grounds. He was surprised the Powers left it. Prime farm ground. Or maybe the property wasn't worth the trouble to raze and rill. Maybe they couldn't find the right ones and zeroes to program into the bots to do the job.

Or maybe the land wasn't needed to feed the less dense populous of Planet Earth.

The lot only held twenty cars in the first place—plenty of space for the regulars and the twice-a-year overflow crowd at Christmas and Easter. Theirs was a quiet town. Even quieter now that Hiram and Gabe were about the only souls left. A few families dotted the county, and a few other churches still stood.

Or leaned.

Empty. But they served as archaeological signposts of things gone by.

But mostly folks, even good country lovin' ones who adored the land (even their high-tech kiddos at that point had at least a mite's leg-worth of respect for it) and had lived it and worked it for generations, bailed from not-on-the-map towns like Sadler when the drones came to do the farming.

When the Powers That Be harvested their lands for them, removing the germy human contagion element. After they harvested everything Hiram Lloyd knew about farming to program the bots to do their bidding and feed the country. Well, what was left of the country.

Hiram strolled to the side of the church and leaned a shoulder on the siding. He took the toothpick—one he'd made himself from scraps of the fallen birch tree in his back yard—from behind his ear and worked it around in his mouth. Glory hated when he did that. Told him he'd for sure choke and puncture his esophagus.

Morning glories in white and cobalt blue climbed and wiggled over the shrubbery and up the sides of the church. Too bad that when the time came later on, their blossoms will have retreated with the rising sun.

He never listened to her. Would just grin and go on. Though back then, their toothpicks were purchased from a bi-monthly run to the store…

The landscape shrubbery, once a project he and Glory had taken on with gladness, threatened to overrun the foundation. Green shoots and spindly twigs and runners went this way and that, reaching and groping for whatever they could hold on to. Much like Hiram's beard and hair. Only his was white and not green. Likely, in places, the roots had wormed their way through the concrete and brittle windowpanes and were peeking into the basement of Sadler Christian Fellowship wondering what those relics were stacked in the corners.

Pianos.

Pew benches in need of repair.

Wooden offering plates with their red felt bottoms lookin' like smashed top-hats.

Hymn books piled and scattered.

Books. What were those? Everyone nowadays has a screen for everything.

Even Hiram. He pulled his phone from his overall's front pocket. No notifications. Gabe was on his way. The gear and the notifications to the community—what was left of it—went out late last night. He knew he'd be taking a huge risk with this, but Hiram hoped he could reach just a few.

Reach a handful a generation once or twice removed to show them the power of kindness. To resurrect a long-since-forgotten custom.

The power of human connection.

And, by the ache in his bones and the pull in his heart, Hiram needed to do this before he became a pile of ashes to scatter across this lot to join his sweet Glory.

A V-formation of seven bots flew overhead, their metal appendages hanging off in all directions. Some for planting, some for spraying. Others sporting digital eyeballs to keep an eye on things. The Powers That Be on the other side of those feeds had never bothered with Hiram. He did what he was told. And they let him pitter and dither around with his John Deere and clear-blue sky trips to the church.

Hiram was a good citizen. Raised Gabe under the code of no contact. Poor kid. Tethered to technology from the time he was a baby. Likely would marry a woman equally tethered and their babies would be of the test-tube-laboratory sort as opposed to the good-old-fashioned sheet-tangling sort.

Hiram wrung his hands together, feeling the knots and realizing here under the morning light that his darkening age spots were not exactly spots, haaving taken over most of his hands' pigments. Hiram wanted more than anything, before his passing, to show Gabe a real connection. Give him a glimpse of the good ol' days when people were human and not, well, not whatever they are now.

Poor Gabe was so brainwashed by the Powers that the tot wouldn't even shake Granddad Hiram's hands in the privacy of their own home. Not even when Hiram tried to make a game of it. "Hands should be covered at all times, Granddad." Gloves and mittens and even paraffin wax dips were all the rage.

Took the boy a long time to even let Hiram wrap an arm around his shoulder and give a little squeeze…

How Hiram missed a good, strong embrace.

But mostly Hiram missed the handshakes. The nonverbal agreement that country folks had with one another. The greetings of strangers and family and friends alike. A firm grim and a slap on the back. Closeness. Connection.

Some days he was glad Glory hadn't lived past the virus. She'd have not liked this no-touch stuff. Cuddler she was. Mother and grandmother to all in the community.

Those bright and rainy and snowy and humid Sunday mornings. All of them. All of them were her favorites. She'd stand with Hiram on the stoop at the double-door entry to the church. Pastor Dickey'd stand across from them. And the three of them would hand-shake and greet each person. Hugs often. Kisses sometimes.

But always, always a handshake and a look-'em-in-the-eye greeting, and Glory would know off the bat if someone had good news. Bad news. Didn't sleep. Lost someone.

Or just wasn't right with the good Lord that mornin'. She'd give Pastor Dickey a wink and he'd be on it and straighten it all out by Sunday dinner.

Grace just knew.

All with a handshake.

Hiram wasn't bad at it. He did his fair share of winkin' at the pastor on that front stoop over the years, but Glory…Glory just knew.

When Hiram explained to Gabe what he wanted to do, the boy went whiter than a ghost, but agreed. The kid did have a bit of Glory in him…he was intuitive, even if he was raised in the Drone age. Gabe had studied Hiram's face. Looked deep into his Granddad's eyes and Hiram recognized a glimmer of Glory. That intuitive knowing.

And Gabe caved and sent out an anonymous digital invite with the GPS coordinates to Sadler Christian Fellowship and the start time of the Handshake Revival.

Hiram fished the front door keys from his pocket. Not that anyone would want access to the old church building, but good steward that he was, he kept it locked up just like between services in the place's hay days when little kids put on the nativity in the winter and hunted eggs—hard boiled ones all dyed with vinegar and colorings in the ladies' kitchens—in the spring. Glory and Hiram would let the grass grow up a little taller for the egg hunt, give the kiddies a bit more of a challenge while moms and dads and grandparents snapped their film or videotaped. Hiram would mow it nice and neat down proper the Monday after while Grace washed communion cups and straightened the hymnals… The good 'ol days.

He swung the front door open. He'd not been inside for quite a few months. Too many memories. After images and memory ghosts floated through the sanctuary, mingled with the dust motes swirling in the morning rays the dirty windows allowed through. The wooden pews stood firm, waiting for warm bodies. The pulpit waiting for Dickey and God to work their magic. The aisle begged for sinners come home to journey to the front and testify. Shake Pastor's hand afterward and forever have a home in heaven and a home church in Sadler.

Behind the pulpit, the baptistry had long dried up, evaporating come-to-Jesus water left a rim of calcium deposits that still hugged the tub's top. White robes hung from hooks, never to be worn again.

Unless there's a revival.

It was a cryin' shame—quite literally, Hiram cried—that he'd had to explain to Gabe what a revival was.

At any rate, the directions were clear. Simple. Even a drone could follow them (though Hiram prayed to God Almighty that the drones would be so far out over the crops that their prying metal lenses wouldn't catch sight of what was going down at Sadler Christian Fellowship).

He walked on through one of the tiny Sunday school classrooms toward the side door that faced the parking lot, and he unlocked it. In one door. Out the other. A quick, painless connection that proved it could be done.

In honor of Glory and Dickey and Will and so many others who'd come in the front. Sat in the pews, left out the side and were loving and kind and connected.

The invite? Come as you are.

Come with gloves or those blasted Digi-Digits or paraffin wax or Aunt Bessie's mustard-yellow knitted mittens. But, better yet, bring your bare-naked hands. Experience firsthand, no pun intended, the ethereal sensation of a genuine handshake and a how-do-you-do, country style.

Hiram heard Gabe's vehicle coming down the road. He motioned for his grandson to pull next to the tractor. Leave room for the others to park. If there were any others that responded to the invitation.

Gabe met Hiram at the side door. "Hey, Granddad." No offer of a handshake or embrace. Love in his eyes, love in his voice. But no contact. As per the Powers That Be and their brainwashing stupidity.

"Are we ready? You ready?" Hiram looked down at their hands— his bare ones and Gabe's covered ones. Gabe wrung his together under the blue nitrile gloves. Usually Gabe wore something a little thicker. Maybe the kid was trying.

"Yeah, Granddad. Let's see what happens." The men walked to the front stoop. Hiram took his old position at the open door, leaning against the handrail of the steps. Gabe, unknown to him, stood in Pastor Dickey's spot opposite.

They stood in quiet for a bit. Hiram listened for incoming drones but heard no electric-techno buzz above him nor from behind the church. They had at least a few minutes. If only the two of them, Hiram hoped to get Gabe to ditch the gloves and give a proper, manly handshake before the afternoon was up.

Hiram wasn't sure what Gabe was thinking. Kid looked nervous, like he was straining to hear any buzz or whirl or sirens to barrel down. Likely he thought Granddad had lost all the rest of his marbles —few the ancient man had left—and he was simply trying to honor the fuzzy memories and stories told of Grammaw Glory.

Then an engine broke the silence. Not a drone buzz. Not a newer-than-yours vehicle. But a good old-fashioned truck. Pickup by the sound of it. As it came into view and slowed in front of the church, Hiram made out Pastor Dickey's son and his wife driving Dickey's old Ford Ranger. Hiram beamed. Gabe gawked. They pulled in on the other side of Hiram's John Deere and met the men at the stoop.

Without saying a word, and with only a smile on his face, Hiram held out his bare-naked hand, age spots and arthritis knots and all. Dickey Jr. did the same. Bare handed.

And the first handshake in Sadler for two decades went down in the books. Hiram let the tears run. He was ready for that bubble of emotion. Knew it would happen and drew out the hankie Glory had sewn for him from a panel of old, blue curtains back in the day.

Dickey Jr.'s wife, not so brave, had on mittens, but took her shake with a shaky smile. They nodded at Gabe, clearly picking up on the cue that the young Lloyd wasn't quite ready for *that* level of interaction, but gave no judgement. How could they? All humans were a mess of one sort or another.

The couple went inside and sat in the front row and looked around the musty, dusty church.

Gabe stared wide-eyed at his grandfather.

"And that, my dear boy, is how it's done." Hiram stuffed the hanky back in his pocket, peeked in at the couple, and leaned against his handrail.

Another engine. This time the Willaby's from down by Sadler Creek. Three generations. The older ones took their shake, the younger, about ten years younger than Gabe, felt more comfortable with Gabe and refrained from shaking, but all three Willaby's found a pew and just sat. Happy with their connection.

Another engine.

Another family. Mixed reactions. Mixed connections, but connections nonetheless.

As the day went on, Gabe worried about being fined for gatherings over one hundred. Hiram pointed out most were in their cars, and the sanctuary barely held seventy, so they'd be fine. Gabe worried about not washing up between contacts. Gabe worried about lots and lots of things, but Hiram pointed out that no drones were in sight on this beautiful clear-blue sky day with the dainty breeze sent from God Almighty and Glory herself.

And Gabe finally stopped voicing such complaints, as the crowd wouldn't allow such time.

And Hiram and his grandson watched as family after family, car after pickup, after tractor—yes, a few good old-fashioned tractors—filled the lot, filled the stoop, shook, or didn't shake (either was fine), and took a seat. When the church filled, the front rows, without direction and without prodding, just knew—knew like Glory—it was time to move on through the little Sunday school classroom with its tiny metal chairs and short-to-the-floor table and flannel graphs of Jesus healing the sick and Moses parting the sea dotting the wall. And they'd leave out the side door to their vehicle and be on their way.

Twice, ladies, unasked and unprodded, after they'd received their handshake—bare-naked ones or not—saw the need for Gabe and Hiram to eat. Dinner on the grounds, so to speak, showed up in ham sandwiches and pots of coffee. Even the grumpiest one in Sadler—old Mrs. Shaw—got over herself and baked the boys oatmeal cookies with raisins and chocolate chips.

Connections. Like the good ol' days.

Hiram's heart was full. The traffic slowing, but still steady on the old country road. He and Gabe barely had time for a conversation between the two of them for all the folks coming to the revival.

The sun was dipping, though, and the farmer drones would be flying back to their bases for a charge and a clean and a download of their memory banks. The traffic slowed a bit, and Hiram had time to focus on Gabe in between greeting folks.

"Well, what do you think?" Hiram rubbed his sore hands. They were sore when the day started, now he could barely stand the touches, but he'd continue as long as there were ones willing to greet him.

"I think you're in pain, Granddad. I think…" Gabe looked down at his gloved hands and toyed with the edges of the nitrile. He stuck his head inside and took in the pew-fulls of people. "I think…"

Gabe shrugged and brushed a tear on his shoulder. He pulled one glove off. Then another.

And he shook Granddad Hiram's hand for the first time. Ever.

Hiram couldn't hold back the tears and allowed his shoulders to shake unashamed with sobs. He didn't even bother digging out the hanky. The men hugged. A tiny line formed on the stoop of the church, but all waited patiently.

And all wept with the men. Those that had on gloves or mittens or Digi-Digits removed their coverings.

Down to the bare-naked knuckles and nude palms.

"I think I need to take over. I think you need a rest."

"I think you'll be okay, Gabe. I think you'll be okay." He offered Gabe his hanky.

Gabe paused. "Uh…"

Hiram laughed. "Baby steps. Baby steps. Grammaw Glory has an entire dresser drawer full in my nightstand. That's where they'll be… Toothpicks too."

Gabe nodded and smiled. And faced the line with his own bare-butt naked hands.

Hiram took his leave, from the stoop, and all the folks in line just knew. And understood.

Hiram sat in his dear John Deere cab and watched the cars trickle to and from the parking lot, watched the people go in the front and out the side door. He closed his eyes and pictured the whites and cobalts of morning glories that would blossom out in the morning, in the bright new dawn over Sadler Christian Fellowship.

And he knew Glory'd be so, so pleased with her only grandson and her dear Hiram Lloyd's Handshake Revival.

Just Enough

The responsibility of caring for elderly grandparents has Lacey torn between her loyalty toward them and wanting to live her own life. Will this be the couple's last holiday in their beloved country home, or will Lacey find just enough hope to keep going?

Lacey had just enough sleep to know she needed to brush her teeth, but not enough sleep to notice the difference between the tubes of Crest and Neosporin. She froze the toothbrush a mere centimeter from her lips, ever so thankful that she caught her error before smearing antibiotic ointment all over her incisors. She rinsed the bristles under the cold tap water.

Well water, to be more precise. The tiny country house had only this one tiny bathroom, so she was always in a hurry lest someone else urgently needed the facilities.

And lately, someone always needed the facilities. Grandma was up coughing twice, which was her normal. Grandpa was up to the bathroom three times, also normal. Sleep was not easy when the spare bedroom was directly on top of theirs, and, even when the old couple were simply snoring in sync, every noise and thump worked its way up the air ducts or reverberated through the floorboards directly under Lacey's bed.

Built by her grandfather decades before, this house was a safe haven for her and her mother when her father split, leaving them with an expensive apartment they couldn't afford and tax problems galore. As a young girl, the upstairs bedroom had held all kinds of magic and mischief with unique cubbies and closets and built-in odd shelving. She'd press her ear to the floor and against the vents in various places to catch snippets of "adult" conversation.

Fifteen years later, her mother passed—Grandma and Grandpa's only child. At the time, Lacey didn't fully grasp what this meant. The care and keeping of the ornery pair would fall to her. But not before Lacey, grown to a young adult and no longer interested in eavesdropping or magic, and equally in a hurry to shed all things elderly and antiquated, moved to Lewisville. A big city compared with a populous of thirteen thousand as opposed to the tiny country burg (with its one full stop sign that most Oldenburg ignored) of a mere two-hundred-and-nineteen.

Of which two hundred always knew her business.

The "big city" adventure of freedom and independent living lasted all of four years before Gran and Gramps started showing signs of slowing down. At first she thought they simply disapproved of her boyfriends. All two of them.

One was a lawyer, promising and gallant. Grandpa had warned her that was all he'd be. A lawyer, and Lacey would be an add-on to his life. Grandma nodded her approval and added, "You need a guy that's just a guy. Yeah, he needs a job and such, but that shouldn't be his identity." Much to Lacey's chagrin, her grandparents had been spot-on. Mr. Perfect Lawyer dude was all law with not enough love to balance even simple request of time spent together with his high-and-mighty career.

The second guy, a med student on his way to becoming a world-class hand surgeon, ended in much the same way. With a precursor warning from her grandparents.

Lacey came to realize they weren't ploying to get her to make the trek to Oldenburg to spend more time with them. They truly cared.

Then they truly needed her to spend more time with them.

Alone, no connections and a job that traveled, Lacey couldn't say no. She's all they have.

She brushed and swished—Crest for sure—and spit out the minty froth, washing it down the drain. Lately, she'd been spending more and more time in this tiny country house taking care of her grandparents. Her editing job allowed her the freedom to leave Lewisville with its not-nearly-fast enough internet and spend several nights here—sans internet—to accomplish household tasks the older couple just couldn't handle.

And the tasks grew and grew with each passing month.

One more holiday season, just keep them in their own home and together for one more season…

Lacey knew this would likely be the last—or next-to-the-last— holiday set that she'd spend here caring for them. She felt this reality sink in while taking down their tree with all the red bird decorations. Dozens of birds, all beak-to-beak. And while taking down the greeting cards sent by dozens of neighbors that Grandma had taped all over the door frames. With each pack up of a red or green bauble, or pair of birds, Lacey knew it might be the last time.

Next season, she'd likely be busting them out on day passes to go to her little apartment, this country home long-sold, but she couldn't handle the chores and them alone. Long-term-care facilities were full up at the moment, but, unknown to her grandparents, Lacey had been researching them and had one picked out—one that would take a husband-wife duo of fifty years—just as soon as a double room opened.

Her gut knotted. No one, and she knew absolutely no one, would think her grandparents to be as great as she thought they were, despite their quirkiness. She tried to push the thought of that awful, impending conversation out of her mind. She had things to do and would not discuss such things with her beloved grandparents right after the holidays. *Just a few more months. If only I could handle them alone for a few more months…*

She slid her "Grandma's House" toothbrush into its holder. Hopefully she'd not have to use this toothbrush tomorrow. Hopefully the morning would go smoothly and she could return to her apartment after four long days of extra "holiday helping" on top of her standard weekend tour coming up.

She exited the bathroom after tying up her brown hair into her "work-time" messy ponytail, and was in the kitchen in four steps. The living room was just off the kitchen and housed the wood stove—the only source of heat the old couple would tolerate, unless someone was heating up the kitchen with the cookstove baking turkey or boiling a huge pot of chili soup.

Lacey shivered as she looked out the window and wiggled her feet inside her fuzzy socks. The naked locust trees whipped in the wind. A couple of sparrows dug at the ground, hoping for a snack. A male cardinal, bright and glorious flitted in the treetop, calling for its mate. A light dusting of snow had accumulated last night, and rogue spits of it would rise a few inches off the ground and swirl around. Likely, ice lurked underneath the white. She'd have to give stern warnings to Grandpa about not attempting to make a run to the wood pile behind the house.

She started a pot of coffee and preheated the oven. She whipped up a batch of banana oat muffins—doubling the ingredients so they could have breakfast with no fuss tomorrow, as well. After sliding the muffin tins into the oven, she sat at the table and moaned as she realized she'd missed some of the Christmas décor. The tablecloth had been used since Thanksgiving, and she'd missed it in yesterday's decoration tear-down.

The tiny oak table still wore the green tablecloth with the embroidered Christmas cardinals, sitting beak-to-beak on a branch complete with sequined pinecones. Grandma hadn't made this particular piece with her own hands, but the lady who did make it was a good friend and long dead, and therefore, the cardinals came out each year, giving Lacey just that much more laundry and packing away after the festivities.

She sighed again as she traced the lovebirds. At least the birds had each other to keep them company until next season.

Sometimes the decorations just became part of the backdrop. And of the hundreds of trips from the living room through the kitchen and back again, the green and red bird cover had melted out of her view, becoming one with the table, unnoticed a mere day or two after Thanksgiving until someone slopped coffee or gravy on it and it needed washed.

The landline rang. Lacey jumped up, intent on grabbing it before it woke up her grandparents, but it was too late. She heard Grandpa's raspy morning voice barking at whoever was on the other end. Lacey went into their bedroom. They slept in separate twin beds, and Grandma had swung her feet out of the covers and was sitting, rubbing her eyes, and reaching for her oxygen tubing hooked to a green cylindrical tank at the foot of the bed. Lacey rolled her eyes. Grandma was supposed to wear it all the time…

Grandpa was still supine, phone to ear. "—don't need no more tanks. She'll be okay."

"Grandpa, who is it?"

He didn't even bother covering the receiver. "It's that nut-job of an oxygen company. We don't need no more tanks. She's full up."

Grandma had required oxygen after her last flare-up of congestive heart issues. Grandpa was holding a grudge due to the last delivery driver being, well, a bit rude and gruff. The complaints abounded from the brute of a woman as she set up and swapped out Grandma's tanks.

Complaints about the roads. The weather. How all the "country folks" all needed oxygen at the same time, and this wasn't her normal route. Unprofessional, yes, but the options for delivery companies were slim to none out here. "Gramps, it can't hurt to have a backup set, especially in the winter."

He moaned and said into the phone "I said no—"

Lacey yanked the phone from his hand—a phone she'd purchased for the pair five years ago. They still had a landline. Cells were nearly useless all the way out in Oldenburg. At least they'd updated to a cordless set, with receivers in the bedroom and the living room. "This is Lacey, I'm Mr. and Mrs. Cobble's granddaughter. Yes. Yes. Please send someone today—"

"We don't need—"

"Granddad, hush. Never mind him. I said we could use the extra tanks, especially if you've got a driver willing to come out all this way. Yes. Thank you." Lacey pushed *END* and handed him back the receiver to place on the charging cradle. "Funny how the lady who *actually* needs the oxygen didn't speak up."

"Oh, honey. I just don't think about it, that's all." Grandma coughed again as she adjusted the nose piece and breathed deeply. "Hey. That feels better. I should wear this more often."

Lacey moaned as she went back to the kitchen to tend to the muffins. She pulled the oven door open, greeted by a waft of burnt banana muffin smoke.

And this why Lacey has her hands all the way full.

Rick checked his GPS, but all he could see was his reflection in the black screen reminding him he needed to trim his beard. With no signal in these parts, the app had frozen. As frozen as the icy roads all around. Salt trucks, few and far between the further one got from Lewisville, had perhaps made one simple pass right down the middle of the country road. Maybe. Or maybe the grit he heard under his tires was just more icy chunks.

He readjusted himself in the driver's seat of the panel van and gripped the wheel a little more firmly, thankful it was still daylight. His other oxygen deliveries were complicated—from icy driveways to insurance payment issues, Rick had his hands full all morning and was now three hours behind schedule for the Cobbles on Rock Haven Road.

He should've started with Mrs. Cobble, if his predecessors' experience with Mr. Cobble had been relayed accurately. Apparently, the man was a little more than snarky and didn't like intrusions—even of the life-saving variety. "Be prepared to duck," the last driver, Becky, had told him.

Becky quit when asked to work overtime for the holidays on this route. Rick had nowhere else to be and was glad to help. He banked the overtime dough for a nicer place. Maybe someplace tucked around one of these windy country turns. Mostly, he was content to bounce along in quiet solitude for the most part, though, once in a while, he'd like someone along for the ride—whether in the delivery van or life in general—to share a thought with.

No, he didn't mind days like this, holiday season or not. He may as well be alone on the cold road as to be alone in an equally chilly apartment.

"Turn right in fifty feet," The robotic lady updates her directions, but five miles too late. He'd passed that turn a while back.

"Too late. Already ahead of you."

The screen glitched, the signal finally reaching the rural county and his not-so-trustworthy comrade barked, "Your destination is in one mile."

"Your destination is in 800 feet."

"Your destination is in 500 feet."

He reached for the windshield wipers to try to clear the icing condensation off the windshield. He'd have to tell the company the van's defrost was going out.

"Your destination is in 300 feet."

"Alright, already." He reached up a second time to kill the navigation nag, but before he could, just as the window had cleared enough to see clearly, a rabbit popped out of the adjacent ditch and hopped in front of him. He yanked the steering wheel hard to the left, skidding into a yard, barely missing the mailbox and then turned hard to the right to miss the cement well cap. Rick tried to turn into the spin, to get the van to straighten, but the grass was so caked with ice, his van twisted until he was again facing the road and the mailbox sporting the name Cobble and the numbers 3201.

"You have reached your destination. 3201 Rock Haven Road, Oldenburg."

"No kidding, Einstein." Rick exhaled, put the van in park, and prayed the Cobbles hadn't seen what happened.

And that the oxygen tanks hadn't come loose from their straps in the tussle.

After a breakfast of semi-burnt muffins and after the kitchen was cleaned, Lacey yanked the tablecloth from its spot as Grandma yapped at her to be careful when she washed it. "Delicate, dear, delicate cycle." Lacey should've left to go home by now. Back to the big city. Back to the peace of her apartment. But alas, the impromptu oxygen delivery would keep her tied up in the country until the tanks were set up, stored, and Grandpa stopped his raving about the interruption.

In the meantime, she busied herself with chores to lighten their load. She lugged the Christmas tote down from the cubby, ready to store away the tablecloth once it had completed its tumble through the washer and dryer.

Her grandparents had settled into the living room to watch the morning news and then drift in and out of snoozing as daytime television marched across the screen. She tried to slip on her coat and slip out the door for the woodpile quietly, but Grandpa caught her when a commercial break came on a little louder than the programming.

"You'd better wear your new slip-ons, honey."

"That's okay, Grandpa, I'll stay in the grass."

Grandma stirred next, and not missing a beat, joined her husband in the warning lecture. "We got you those for a reason, dear. We don't want you falling down."

They referred to the Christmas gift they'd ordered for Lacey from a junk-mail catalog. Slip-on ice cleats, perfect for any shoe and any size foot. They'd even cut out the advertisement, with the price of the cleats neatly marked through with one of Grandma's rollerball blue ink pens. They were so proud. Lacey couldn't help but love them all the more for the thoughtful, although never-gonna-use-it gift.

"That's okay, guys. It'll just take a minute."

"It'll take two seconds to fall on your rear, dear."

Lacey smiled and nodded to the television where their show had started up again. Like toddlers with Barney the dinosaur, they were once again glued to the daytime talk show host.

Lacey slipped on her coat, ignored the shiny new ice cleats and stepped outside into the brisk air. Most dry days, Lacey's grandfather could manage to bring in a small armful of firewood. Lacey would come on the weekend and stock the indoor holder up, clean out the ash bin and not worry too much. But only on the dry days, and today —likely the next several days—weren't going to be dry. The sky grew grayer by the hour and she could feel the heaviness in the air—likely freezing rain.

She really had to get moving and get back to town before the weather turned.

As she stepped into the grass, a panel van came barreling into the drive, narrowly missing the mailbox and well, spun, and then came to a stop in the yard.

The driver stepped out of the car, a broad-shouldered younger guy —not the "brute of a woman" Grandpa had described from the last delivery. He took two steps toward her, mumbling apologies and shaking his head as if stunned. She feared him to be injured and took two steps toward the fiasco to see what she could do to help. On the third step, her boot bottoms failed to grip the ice-coated grass, and she fell on her rear, legs bent awkwardly and arms nowhere near ready to break her fall. Her work-time ponytail came undone on the way down to the ground spraying brown curls all in her face.

And it took only two seconds.

∼

Rick got out of the van and reached the young lady, holding a hand out for her. "I'm so, so sorry. If I'd been more careful, I'd not have spun out in your yard and you'd have been safely on your way to, to—" Rick looked around to see where she may have been headed before his rude arrival. Before he became the reason she might be hurt. "Are you okay? Let me help."

"It's okay. I should've listened. They got me grips, but—" She allowed him to take her hands, soft and small and wet with the melty slush, and pull her to her feet. A slight frame, brown curls in all directions and soft brown eyes to match. A faint hint of banana fell from her locks. Rick had to catch himself from outright staring and force the conversation.

"Grips?" He steadied her by her elbows as she pushed the hair out of her face.

"Yeah, for my shoes, but I didn't—" She stopped mid-sentence. She stared at his feet. At his slip-on ice hugging cleats that his dad insisted he needed if he were to keep with a job like this. "Grips." She stepped back carefully, grinned and pointed to his shoes. His face flushed, more so than it already had been after the spin-out.

"Yeah. My dad was worried."

"My grandparents. But I didn't listen. I should listen. They're always right." She nodded toward the house. "I'm Lacey. You must be from Lewisville Oxygen."

"Yeah. I'm Rick. And I mean, yeah, just Rick. I mean. Yes. I'm Rick. I'm from the oxygen place. Are you good?" He needed to take a step back. Many steps back. Toward his van. Toward the job at hand. And quit thinking about the lovely young lady in front of him. She was grinning at him. Her cheeks flushed—he couldn't tell if from embarrassment or the chill in the air. He didn't feel chilly at all.

"Well, I'll let you get to it, then, just Rick from the Oxygen place. I'll leave the door open. Come in when you're ready." She was brushing chunks of ice off from her pants. "And don't mind my grandfather."

He nodded and went to his van, watching her waddle like a penguin through the grass back toward the house as he slid the panel door open. He forced himself to look inside, very glad that the Cobble oxygen tanks hadn't worked loose during the skid. When he looked back over his shoulder, Lacey had already disappeared into the house.

~

"—told you to wear them, honey."

"Yes, I know this." Lacey was halfway up the stairs to her little bedroom to change clothes—her butt was covered in melted ice and her pride was melting away and man were his eyes green and kind and—

Get it together, Lacey.

She dug in her duffle for clean jeans and a pullover sweater. She ditched her wet clothes in the corner and determined to save face and show Rick from the oxygen place just how reliable she usually is, she would strap on the cleats and get the firewood as had been the destination before the delivery van came skating into the yard.

She was about to head down the stairs, but she heard the exterior door creak open and the banging and clattering of metal and wheels. Rick was inside now, ready to set up Grandma's new tanks. She hung at the top step as she had so many years ago as a child and waited for the conversation to float up to her.

"—glad you're not that brute of a woman. She didn't know what she was doing." Grandad was saying. A new flush raced across her face, heat from she knew not where, as she was frozen to the bone. *Oh, Grandpa.*

"It's okay, Mr. Cobble. I'll have this set up and ready to go in a jiffy. I just wanted to let you know I skidded into your yard. I—"

Lacey stopped listening as her grandparents began the obligatory "are you okays" and "can we get you anythings" and remembered Rick's jawline and country boy scruff. Though he wasn't an Oldenburg country boy. She'd have known him, and he her, had he been one of the two-hundred-and-nineteen humans in this 'ville.

Really, get it together, girl. You've no time for this nonsense. Two old people. Two houses to take care of, Really. And doing it alone.

She leaned against the doorframe, frozen. A thousand thoughts ran through her mind. Rick. Just Rick. Not a lawyer. Not a doctor. Not too good to wear slip-on ice cleats gifted him by his father. She felt like she knew the man, and they'd literally spend two minutes together. If that. But in that two minutes, she'd been, well, beak-to-beak with him just as one of Grandma's many cardinal decorations.

But she felt like he saw her. Really saw her in that stupid moment outside.

She felt like, for the first time in a long time, she wasn't simply blending in the background.

A pause in the conversation downstairs pulled Lacey from her thoughts. Perhaps he'd gone. Perhaps he'd already set things up and was carefully navigating that monster delivery van back onto Rock Haven Road and was heading west toward Lewisville.

But in the pause, she heard ice hitting the side of the house. The sky must've busted open while she was changing clothes.

God, how long had she been standing at the top of the stairs?

She scaled them down, two at a time, to find Grandma and Grandpa grinning like Cheshire cats. The burnt banana muffins—*good grief, could he smell that when he came into the house? Perhaps he thought Grandma had burned breakfast...*

"Well, that wasn't so bad, now was it? A polite delivery person, and a quick setup, not much to complain about, right?" Lacey spoke too quickly, rushing to put her boots back on—this time wrestling the ice cleats on as the door swung open again and there stood Rick, cradling a giant armful of firewood.

Lacey stood in his way, one boot on with cleats, one boot dangling from her hand, the other hand trying and failing to control the curls that spilled across her face.

"I thought it was the least I could do. Save you the, well, save you the trip, and make up for rutting up the yard."

"Get out of the way, girl," Grandpa said.

Grandma was already heading for the kitchen, dragging her oxygen tubing behind her. "I'll start fresh coffee. You aren't going anywhere anytime soon. Too slick. You'll get the van out of the yard and then put it straight in a ditch. Lacey isn't leaving either. I'd worry myself sick with her on the roads. Make yourself comfortable."

"Where, uh, where would you like this?" Rick adjusted the stack of wood against his chest.

Lacey was mortified. She hopped on her socked foot out of the way, pointing to the firewood holder. He managed to kick his cleated shoes off at the door and began stacking the pieces into the holder.

She took off her one boot and locked up the front door. Rick was already stoking the fire. He still wore his oxygen company's coat, but she could tell he was built even under the extra layers. She tore away from gawking and went to help her grandmother in the kitchen.

The table looked naked without the cardinal tablecloth, and Lacey ran her hands over the oak. "I pulled the tablecloth out of the dryer while you were upstairs." Grandma was still grinning. She handed Lacey the folded linen, the two cardinals showing on top. "This is yours, now."

Lacey must've been upstairs much longer than she'd realized.

"Grandma, I—"

"You can use it here next year. Or at your place. Or at his." Grandma winked and nodded toward the living room where muffled man voices chuckled and jawed over the television. Lacey startled at Grandma's directness and peeked through the doorway to make sure Rick hadn't heard.

"Grandma!"

"He's just a delivery guy, sweetheart. Until you pull him out of the background and make him yours."

"Coffee's done," Grandma called before Lacey could object or argue. Rick now stood in the doorway separating the living room from the kitchen. She held out a mug for him, steam curling above the rim. "Thanks for helping. Sorry you're stuck with us."

"There are worse places to be stuck." Rick took the mug from her but didn't return to the couch. "I see you've taken down most of the decorations already. I've got to get over to my parents to help them with theirs. They always want me to stuff all the stuff back in the attic."

"Most of them? I thought I got all of them."

"Mom and Dad always miss bits here and there, too. Mom says

they blend in and you go holiday-blind to them." Rick took another sip and grinned. "I can help you if you want."

Lacey looked beyond Rick into the living room and didn't see anything she'd missed. She glanced over her shoulder into the kitchen. Aside from the tablecloth, which remained folded neatly on the table, she didn't see anything else.

"Good grief, girl. Look up." Granddad stood in the living room, laughing. Grandma chuckled behind her.

Above Lacey and Rick in the doorway was a single sprig of mistletoe. Two cardinals clung to the sprig, beak to beak. How in the world did she miss that?

Her face flushed fresh all over as Rick handed his mug to Grandpa and reached up to take down the mistletoe. Just Rick from the oxygen company.

He saw her. She wasn't blending in. She didn't need to be alone.

He handed the sprig to Lacey and smiled.

Their fingers brushed. Just a little bit.

But just enough.

Four Seconds

After Oscar loses his long-time mentor, a Civil War battlefield photographer, he's left with an impossible decision. Will Oscar follow his mentor's loyalty to the South or will he forge a new path with new possibilities...

Oscar George rummaged through his darkroom chemicals and wiped a bead of sweat from his brow. Tennessee falls are gorgeous, but the early November Indian Summer and the meager ventilation in the boarding house offered no forgiveness from the heat and even less space for his supplies. It was not yet midmorning and already the sun was promising to be foe, not friend.

Bottles of wet plate solvents and fixing agents clanked together in the wooden storage cabinet with the not-level shelving. A pile of haphazardly folded darkout cloths tumbled around Oscar's feet. A stack of glass plates toppled, thankfully landing on the mass of fabric, and only two chipped. Nevertheless, finding supplies locally will be impossible, and having them couriered not only risky, but unlikely.

And supplies he would definitely need to deal with Mr. Bartholomew Barker's portrait orders. Oscar couldn't afford to be so careless.

The only item he had successfully packed so far this morning was the camera and tripod. At least he'd had enough sense not to hitch up Corncob to the wagon yet. Mr. Umbry had once hitched her before the wagon was fully packed and secured. The sudden outbreak of musket shots over the ridge at the Battle of Belmont spooked the chestnut mare. A Missourian-born photographer, Mr. Umbry was bound and determined to document every aspect of the Union's horrors against the Confederacy. Corncob, his beloved horse (sometimes Oscar wondered if he loved that horse more than Oscar or photography), kept Mr. Umbry from succeeding in that endeavor, her skittish nature toppling over the chemical box and shattering the putrid colloidal mixtures. The wagon floor will be permanently stained from the ordeal, and poor potbellied Mr. Umbry took the lost opportunity with bitter rage.

"Oscar, my boy. I've taught you well. Everything I know. But damned if I didn't forget to tell you not to hitch the horse until you're ready to ride." He'd taught Oscar everything he knew about capturing images and preserving them. That the plates must be kept wet. That the subject matter must be focused first. That the sun could be your best friend or your worst enemy. That day, Mr. Umbry taught Oscar how to clean the mess up without exposing himself to toxic photography fumes.

Oscar gathered the plates and cloths, laid them on his unmade bed, and sat, staving off the uprising of still-fresh grief. Mr. Umbry had taken Oscar in as an apprentice and played the role of father to the boy for years after Oscar's parents died of typhoid. The pair had enjoyed grand travels—albeit with Corncob at the helm—and met such intriguing people. Diplomats, politicians, and socialites.

Then the War.

And Mr. Umbry went from a reasonable soul to hell-bent on documentation. Oscar understood the importance. Everything these days held extreme importance.

Mr. Umbry's reputation grew throughout the South. The impeccable quality of his portraits of Generals and Confederate soldiers and his stills of the battlefield aftermath gave a boost to the local Confederates. The images were used to garner funds from the wealthy and, for those with no means, the pictures gave purpose to carry on. The South must succeed.

Oscar rose and examined himself in the dull washstand mirror. In another time, he'd been filling out nicely, Mr. Umbry's occupation provided well for them. Not so much now. His face was thinner, his dark curls wayward, and his blue eyes looked like those of the soldiers he'd pass along his route. The War claimed lives and light.

He poured water into the basin from the pitcher and splashed his face. A wooden crate under the washstand held Mr. Umbry's photographs that were prepped and ready to be delivered to some of the local business owners—or their wives, rather. He bent and took the lid off the crate and sat on the floor cross-legged. He was going to be late to the Barker's, but he could always blame it on the road blockades and influx of soldiers in Chattanooga's streets.

He thumbed through the first few photos. Shots of married couples. Shots of an old man with his hunting dog.

He paused at the Barker's last family portrait shot. It took Mr. Umbry nearly three hours to wrangle the group, pose them, mediate arguments, and focus the camera, and have them hold the required four seconds for the exposure to take. The plates went dry three times.

He told Mr. Barker that he would leave the job if he didn't get his brood under control and no reputable photographer would ever step foot at the Little White House ever again. Not wanting to be spoken ill of in any business or social circle, vain Mr. Barker laid down the law, and his family finally cooperated.

In the photo, Mr. Barker was seated on a grand plush chair—red, if Oscar remembered correctly. Around him were four sons, spry and healthy. Alive. Before the War.

Four daughters, all young and somber. Curls peeking from under their bonnets. All family members finally posed long enough to capture a nice portrait. All but the youngest girl, maybe seventeen, who defiantly refused to put on her bonnet, her mouth upturned and her head tilted to the side in a dare. Oscar remembered thinking how brave she must be to defy her father—and the social norms.

He fanned through more of the photos. One wealthy family, all since deceased, had ordered portraitures of their slaves. Oscar paused on this image. Their eyes were so different from those of the whites. The lens captured a depth of sadness that passersby would never notice. Because they never dared look passerby in the eyes.

Since the photo, their master passed, leaving them in a will, albeit unknown to the original owners, to a sympathizer, Mr. Henderson.

Oscar inhaled, held his breath for a count of four, and exhaled slowly. From his trouser pocket he took a note. Troop movements. Command base locations. Snippets of conversations he'd collected while on deliveries and shoots. After a while, no one remembers the camera man is in the room, especially when he's busy with wash buckets and foul-smelling chemicals.

He tucked the tiny piece of paper with its cipher between the photo and the copper frame, ensuring that the frame laid flat against the cardboard all around and replaced the image with the others in the box. He fanned them back and forth. From his inspection, he couldn't tell that one package of photos looked any different from the rest. Satisfied, he replaced the lid to the crate and lifted it to the bed with the plates and darkout cloths. He returned to the cabinet and packed the chemicals into the travel case.

Oscar began making trips out to the wagon. Soldiers passed him on each load. He left the wagon unattended long enough to retrieve Corncob from the stall. As he hitched her, two soldiers asked him his business. They pulled the fabric back from the back of the wagon. "What's all this?"

For the third time that week, Oscar enlightened another pair of soldiers on his profession. He showed them the wagon's inscription: Mr. Umbry's Photographic Wagon. Umbry had enlisted Oscar's steady hand to paint the letters onto the wooden slats long ago. They'd since lost their shine, like so many things had.

One soldier used his filthy hands to pull the wooden crate to the wagon's edge and opened the lid. Oscar wanted to scream to the man not to touch the photos—because of the dirt and the fear of finding his contraband—but he held his tongue. *Don't draw attention.*

"So you're Mr. Umbry, then? Great man. I've heard of that one. Picture was in the paper of Braggs. Umbry took it then, yes?"

Corncob stomped her front leg impatiently and snorted, her tail whipping back and forth. The Morgan horse was ready to ride. Right now. But Oscar was frozen to the spot at the back of the wagon.

The second soldier pulled out the Barkers' portrait from the collection then returned it. Sweat ran down the back of his neck despite being in fresher air than the rented room offered.

Oscar nodded. "Umbry took it. I'm his apprentice."

"Well, give him our regards."

And before Oscar could correct them, they went on their way. He hadn't realized he'd been holding his breath. He resituated the crate and secured the tarp over the portable darkroom wagon.

He went around the front to pat Corncob's muzzle. She'd held it together and didn't topple the cart. "Good girl. Steady now." In her velvety ear he whispered, "Forgive me Mr. Umbry. A good Confederate you were, loyal to your cause. But your cause is not mine." He ran his hands through Corncob's midnight black mane. "Some things are too important."

~

Felicity lay on her back, staring at her ceiling through the empty frame of her canopy bed. Where once she'd watch the fine-spun lace dance and flitter with the breeze from the window, now she stared at a lone cobweb Ruthy had missed. The day she and Ruthy had to untack the lace from the frame was a sad one. Felicity didn't think herself to be spoiled, but she did enjoy a few nice things. But alas, everyone must make sacrifices for the Confederate cause, and when the textiles ran low, the socialites still needed a way to upgrade their wardrobes—and handkerchiefs.

A soft knock on the door from Ruthy.

"Come in."

"Miss. Mr. Barker is pacing. Wondering why you aren't downstairs with the rest. They gettin' ready, Miss."

Getting ready. For Mr. Umbry's Photographic Wagon to uproot their entire day. Felicity would rather hide up in her room, giving Ruthy her reading lessons. She may donate her lace to the confederates, but she'd give her soul to the North.

"Well, we mustn't keep Daddy waiting."

She slid from the bed, worked on the crinoline, and stepped into her peach dress. Ruthy settled into a chair next to the window and flipped through her reader. The black girl was a year or two older than Felicity, no one was quite sure. Ruthy was a gift for Felicity's fifteenth birthday, a handmaid all her own. As the youngest child, Daddy doted on her more than any of his other offspring and more than overcompensated for his wife's passing. Loved him, she did. But she also despised him. Some days it tore her soul into bits.

But each time she'd catch Ruthy sobbing in the corner of the stables or behind the pantry, disgust over her family's lifestyle shoved the love a little further into the dark.

"Would you mind helping, Ruthy? I wouldn't bother your studies, but this damned curl!" She never asked Ruthy to attend to her like a true handmaid when they were alone. In the main parts of the Little White House, they'd go about as proper lady and servant, but not here. And if, like today, Felicity was to present herself a well and true socialite, she always asked Ruthy for help, never ordered her about like her sisters did their servants.

Ruthy smiled, knowing how much Felicity hated events and loathed photography sessions even more. She helped pin back an unruly blonde strand that Felicity couldn't quite reach.

"Perhaps, Miss, that fine young boy will be back with Mr. Umbry." Ruthy fluffed the fabric and gave a playful tug on the hem of Felcity's dress as she stood.

"Oh, Ruthy. That was ages ago. Besides. Mr. Umbry tragically passed. I heard someone else took his place and they'd likely not keep on such a scrawny boy. Another mouth to feed and all."

"That there boy with the bright blue eyes wasn't too scrawny, Miss." Ruthy giggled.

Felicity turned to her friend and gave her "the look," and Ruthy nodded in understanding. She took a deep breath and left Felicity to herself. That look was part of the code the ladies had worked out, and it was by no means an unspoken rebuke. Sometimes they behaved so much like best friends in private that Felicity feared it would ooze out their pores for the world to see. Their gaiety had to be squelched long before the photographer arrived. The Good Lord only knew what side he was on.

And if he was a spy.

Down in the drawing room, Daddy was mid-way through imparting his hard-earned wisdom to a colleague. Poor Daddy. Trying so hard to fit into a class he didn't belong to. Mother's family came from old money, and in the early days Daddy did his best to bankrupt the estate with bad deal after bad deal.

"—we'll never know the effects. We'll not see profits turn in this decade, maybe two. With all the rebuilding. Our battlefield boys better pick up the pace. The word is the North is pushing this way. What do you hear?" Daddy looked quite dapper standing there by the mantle in his best suit. He'd put on his cufflinks and the chain from his watch dangled from his pocket.

The colleague was about to answer, but when he saw Felicity, he smiled and nodded to her, then looked back at Daddy for permission to continue.

"Aw, she's fine, Roger. Aren't you, my sweetest? But where's your bonnet?"

"I outgrew it years ago, Daddy. Then I donated it." She smiled at Mr. Roger Jones, a wealthy businessman from Nashville. Tall, lanky, and graying around his sideburns. Half Daddy's age but twice hers. "You know. For the cause." This allowed Roger's shoulders to relax and a smile to emerge.

"She's my last unmarried child." Felicity's stomach tightened. Not again. "Beautiful, yes?"

Roger moved in a little closer, offering her his hand. Felicity turned to look at the mantel, leaving him hanging his hand mid-air like a cold mackerel. She'll not be paraded and passed around in courtship for all of Daddy's overaged men determined to lead such barbaric lives.

Daddy took her elbow roughly and whispered in her ear. "Don't start. Not today. He's a railroad man."

Felicity turned toward the man, offering a rushed apology. Daddy made excuses for her to Roger, with all the family's losses, she could become quite emotional. Felicity stifled a growl and turned to focus on the photographs lining the mantel as the men's voices faded into another part of their grand house.

Mr. Umbry had begun visiting their home for portraitures years before the war started. Daddy was so proud of his children. Proud that he'd not squandered all of Mother's money away and could afford to keep up the estate—and to add inventory of the human sort. She gazed into the images, the one right before Mother had passed held her attention. They were all there. In that photo. Two parents. Four sons. Four daughters. Felicity pulled herself away from the mantel and stared out the window. Now one parent was left grieving what the war took. Three of her brothers were dead. Franklin was "likely imprisoned up North."

But everyone knew he was as good as dead.

The photographer couldn't even make his way here in time to capture any of the extended family. Felicity's sisters married off quickly—mostly Railroad Men, as Daddy preferred. But all of them signed up and shipped out to fight. None of them qualified for more than front-line fodder. None of them returned, leaving her sisters little more than second-hand goods in most suitors' eyes. And most suitor's eyes belonged to men too old for war or not fit to fight.

Felicity remained unmarried. Unattached. Despite the flutter she felt at Ruthy's mention of Mr. Umbry's apprentice, what's the point of love when the one you pine for could be in a pine box by next Tuesday?

She ran her index finger over her mother's image, gently. "Oh, Mama. If you could see the Barkers now. What would you think?"

She'd think Felicity a traitor. That's what she'd think. Mama died years before the conflict, and though she was never cruel to the estate's hands, she was always pleased when Daddy procured another. And another.

Felicity played the part her mother would have wanted her to portray. But it was an act. To her core, she despised being an available socialite who helped Daddy host railroad higher-ups and generals and commanders coming through to brag of victories on the bloody battle-fields. She hated that her brothers had given their lives for this. Though they didn't have a choice but to go, they did so with glee in their steps. Daddy's shoulders squared, and the old man stood tall the day they left home.

Had he known how real things would get, perhaps he'd have wept and held his sons a little tighter. Ruthy caught Felicity weeping that day and had crawled into the canopy bed with her and held her tight.

Felicity shook her head, barring back a wave of sorrow. Ruthy. So brave despite her circumstances. Felicity didn't feel brave at all. Not like the woman she'd read about in the papers. Southern papers, of course. One Elizabeth Van Lew. Risking jail and death to run a spy ring. Oh, to be brave enough to hand over secret messages to an imprisoned Yank in a custard pie.

Had Felicity been brave, she'd not have donated that blasted bonnet. She'd have spent her time rocking on the grand balcony above the Little White House's entry where Daddy's guests lingered before leaving, sharing bits and pieces of vital information. Then, she'd have carefully sewn notes into the hems or the ties of that bonnet and found a way to pass it along. Like a custard. To a Yank.

After gathering her limited moxie, she turned to face the day. The Photographic Wagon would be here soon, and the remaining Barkers would stand dutifully for their portraiture. True Confederates and proud Southerners, all.

Well… Almost true. And almost all.

Oscar unhitched the wagon near the front door and tethered Corncob to the closest shade tree nearest the front door of the Barkers' home. Separating the two would assure that Corncob won't upset the delicate solutions and darkroom setup in the back of the wagon.

He retrieved the tripod and wooden camera case and turned toward the Little White House. He hated the nickname the locals had given the property. President Davis lived in and ran the South's affairs from the Confederate White House. Built in the same style but much smaller, the Barkers' home boasted eight grand columns supporting a massive overhang. Directly above the oversized entry door was a balcony wrapped in wrought iron. Mr. Umbry had said the house earned its nickname because of how integral Mr. Barker was to the cause, housing meetings of generals and leaders.

Oscar remembered a strongly worded discussion about how no photographer sane of mind would do portraitures on that balcony with the oak branches whipping light rays this way and that and then run the plates down to the portable darkroom in the wagon. Fixing the images to the plates was time sensitive, and Mr. Umbry was not one for running up and down the staircase for hours on end.

Knowing the goings on under the Little White House's roof, the only good thing about this property was the view. Lookout Mountain rose high above Chattanooga, untouched by man's insignificance. At least for now. Oscar stood for a moment and took in the bright oranges and yellows and fiery reds flowing from the mountain.

Oscar felt in his bones—and had recorded notes on the same, tucked inside the photo frame—that this tiny part of the Appalachians wouldn't remain unscathed for long.

He wrestled his equipment up the front steps, and before he could knock on the door, it opened slowly. The autumn mountain view he'd admired moments ago evaporated, replaced by the most gorgeous creature he'd ever seen.

Oscar froze.

"Well, are you going to set up, Sir, or would you like to stand on the stoop a while longer in this heat?" She smiled at him, her emerald eyes full of spark, the midday sun dancing across the bust of her dress.

In the sepia image he was about to hand over to her father from Mr. Umbry's last visit, standing before Oscar was the young girl with the defiant, uncovered head and proud chin. But those eyes. The sepia didn't do them or her justice.

But time sure had.

He composed himself. "Yes, Miss. I'm Oscar George. I'm—"

"Here to put us through utter agony for hours. Hold still. Don't fidget. Move here. Hold still again. Don't move while I run about and mix this and that and hide under my little cover behind the camera." She smiled again.

"That's about the sum of it."

"Fine then. I'll tell Daddy you're here. You can set up in drawing room. Daddy's waiting in there. His throne is ready."

"Throne?" Oscar followed her through to the drawing room. He vaguely remembered the layout of the house. He vividly recalled those eyes.

"That's what my sisters and I call the chair he sits in while we all line behind him. He's the King of Little White House. We are his loyal servants."

"I see." Oscar hoped his gaze hadn't lingered too long on her face. He needed to stay focused. To be quick and clear headed. Mr. Barker was to host a grand dinner this evening for prominent Chattanooga businessmen. And not all of them as loyal to the South as they appeared. Oscar hoped to draw out the photography session long enough to be able to pass the photo from the wooden crate to the gentleman who bought the family in the portrait.

He certainly didn't need any distractions.

"Hello, young Oscar. My, how things have changed." Mr. Barker offered a firm handshake but then realized Oscar's hands were full.

"Sorry, lad—oh, but you're much too old for lad, now, aren't you? A shame about Mr. Umbry. Just a shame."

Oscar sat the equipment down, wiped his palms on his trousers, and then shook Mr. Barker's hand properly, keeping the young lady in the periphery of his vision. "Yes, sir, and thank you. Mr. Umbry will be missed."

"A real hero. We appreciate his sacrifice."

Oscar, still so torn, nodded and turned to his setup. "I have your portraits from… from before." His hands were so sweaty. Yards away under the oak tree was his act of treason. Yards away from this powerful man with powerful connections.

"Fantastic. Felicity, dear, won't you have Ruthy bring in some iced tea."

Felicity. *That* was her name.

He thought he caught that same look of defiance over the bonnet in her gaze toward her father as she left the room. Oscar wiped his hands again—this time for a completely different reason—and headed for another armful of supplies from the wagon.

Ruthy turned her nose to the air and went about making a pitcher of iced tea when Felicity entered the kitchen and announced Mr. Oscar George was indeed Mr. Umbry's replacement.

Felicity paced behind her friend as the tea boiled and spat, but she didn't know why the nerves. Moments before, she had been reminiscing about her mom and pining to be like Ms. Van Lew. Then she could barely keep her composure once she saw those striking blue eyes.

Oscar George.

The little boy she'd found little more than interesting the last time they'd met had grown into quite the specimen. She smoothed the front of her dress and fussed with the pins in her hair and paced until Ruthy shooed her out of the kitchen. "Miss, you'll ruin yourself before the photos. And before Master's dinner." Felicity moaned as she passed by Alma and Trudy busying with the roast and peeling potatoes. Several empty pie crusts lay draped over the tins waiting for apples and cinnamon. Daddy had begged, pleaded and borrowed from the wealthy around town for the affair to lay such a spread. Said it would further their cause if those in power were well-fed.

She'd pushed the dinner of even more Railroad Rogers completely from her mind, choosing to focus on one horrid task at a time. She'd love to gather information, but to do so, she'd have to play the role of a flirt, but playing incompetent was exhausting. She'd get caught like old Rose Greenhow for sure.

And now there was Oscar. Though he may still be a bit backward, he definitely wasn't a little boy anymore.

She made her way back to the drawing room, where Oscar was adjusting drapes this way and that. His tripod was aimed at Daddy's throne, and two sisters were gossiping by the mantel, removing old photos from their spots. Jenny was about to cry, as recent widows often do. Grace was telling her to keep it together, and Melody couldn't ever bring herself to look at the mantel. She'd married first. Her wedding photo was among the collection.

Felicity took the portrait from them and sat it back in its spot. It was so full of life. They were so full of life. "That's enough of that, ladies. You don't want to look blotchy for Daddy's portrait, yes?"

She remembered back to that day before the war. She remembered how long it took Mr. Umbry to set everything up. Oscar was doing the same now, the top half of his long form tucked under the cloth that hid the camera from the light as he used his foot to tap the legs of the tripod this way and that.

"Mr. George. How long might you be? I'm only asking so as to let Ruthy know whether you'd like your tea now or after," Felicity tried to lighten the mood in the room as her sisters huddled and adjusted hair, hats, hankies, and hoops.

Oscar wriggled from under the cloth and carefully let the edges remain draped over the camera.

"We're about ready, and the light will change soon as the afternoon draws on. We best get started."

"Very good then. Girls, shall we?" Daddy escorted them to the throne.

Dutifully, the four women positioned themselves behind the armchair in order of age as Daddy crossed his legs and rested his arms on the chair. Oscar waited as they fussed and fidgeted about, and then Daddy asked, "Are we good, sir?"

As Oscar ducked under the cloth again, Felicity's mouth went dry. For the next many minutes, she'd be frozen, unable to move anything but her eyes. And her eyes were not obeying her. She wanted to look at where the lens might be—not at his legs.

And definitely not directly into his eyes as he emerged from under the cloth. He caught her gaze, and she smiled a bit, hoping one of her sisters was smiling at him too.

"Felicity, was it Miss?" Oscar approached her. She swallowed hard and nodded ever so slightly, as she couldn't quite remember exactly all the steps in this much-too-long process. "Your dress is out of frame. May I?" Then he paused and gave her a half grin. "You can speak, just don't move too much else."

"Good, Lord, lad. Don't tell her to speak, we'll have no peace!" Daddy jibed, and her sisters all broke into giggles. "Now, now, ladies. We talked about this. We're not to give Mr. George the same hell we gave Mr. Umbry, God rest his soul."

Felicity rolled her eyes. "Yes, Mr. George, do what you must to put us out of our misery."

As the others regained their composure, Oscar put two fingers on Felicity's elbow and ever so gently led her to step in closer to Grace. A much different touch than earlier when Daddy had scolded her. She caught her breath.

"That's fine. That should be good," Oscar said, and Felicity dared not allow her eyes to drift toward him.

He stepped back under the black cloth, and she could see the outline of his hands moving the lens underneath. "That's all perfect, Mr. Barker. Now, please. Remain totally still while I run out to the wagon. This will take a few minutes while I prepare the plate. Usually an apprentice does that part while I do this, so it may take me longer today. My apologies."

"Poor Mr. George. Doing your job and Mr. Umbry's. Best we don't speak then. That's what always gets us into trouble. Total silence, girls. Not a peep," Daddy ordered.

Oscar took long strides out of the room, nearly running.

In the few moments he was gone, Felicity swore her heartbeat could be heard in the silence. Feared its beating would somehow show up as a blur in the photo right over her chest. She willed herself to calm down. Focus on something else. The dinner tonight.

Perhaps she could begin devising a way to help the cause. The right cause, anyway. Her nose began to itch, but she dared not scratch it. The sooner Mr. George was on his way, the sooner she could get back to—

Oscar burst into the room in a full out run toward the camera gripping a black box in his hands. He nearly dove under the black cloth.

"When I remove the cloth and the lens, you must continue to remain perfectly still. Here we go… ready?"

Oscar removed the black cloth.

"Now."

Oscar removed the lens, and for a count of four, Felicity Barker and Mr. Oscar George fixed their gazes on each other until Oscar put the lens back on the camera.

"Can we move now?" Grace asked.

"Yes," Oscar took the slim black case out of the camera and sprinted out of the room once again.

Felicity remained frozen to her spot as her sisters and father stretched and chatted. In four seconds, the camera created an image that would last for generations. In four seconds, Felicity's heart outranked her mind and dreamt a future that wouldn't have a chance of lasting past the next round of musket fire.

Oscar willed his hands to stop shaking and his brow to not drop sweat into the washpan as he poured the colloidal over the plate and tilted it back and forth. As he rinsed the plate, the image of the Barkers slowly emerged.

He'd nearly overexposed the shot. He wanted to draw out the session—not waste supplies.

While he was focusing the group in the frame, he could stare at her without anyone knowing under the safety of the darkout, albeit an upside-down image, but stare nonetheless. But out in the bright drawing room, and right there in front of her remaining family as they all aimed their gazes at the lens, he aimed his at her face.

He'd almost dropped the lens cap at the end.

He finished with the plate and cleaned it up to show Mr. Barker what the final product would be. Allowing himself to look full on at Felicity—and only Felicity—was out of character for him. And so was the thought dancing around in his head that when he got around to making the prints for the family, he'd make one for himself—

"Mr. George, that was quite a smooth process, given you're all alone." Felicity's voice sang out behind him. He turned to find her holding two glasses of iced tea. He placed the plate carefully in the darkroom and took the glass.

"Thank you, Miss."

"Where will you go next?"

I hope not too far. A good Barker brawl in the drawing room before the photo shoot would've helped assure that he could pass the message to Mr. Henderson.

Oscar took a tiny sip of the tea. Maybe he could linger with this glass—and the girl—and moved toward the tree where Corncob stood. One of the stable hands had brought a bucket of water for the mare. Oscar ran his hands through her mane. "Wherever the portrait orders or the war—commands. Things move slow. Troops blocking roads. Roads destroyed. Supplies run low. It all depends."

"Will you follow in Mr. Umbry's example? Battlefield photography?" She looked away from him as she brought her glass to her pink lips and took a long sip.

"More than likely. It's a good cause." He had to be careful. As smitten as he was with her, she could be his downfall before he even got a proper start.

"Isn't it dangerous? Being so close to the battle? I mean, Mr. Um—" She caught herself. "I'm so sorry. How impolite of me."

"That's okay. He knew the dangers. Usually we set up away from the battle. That time, the troops moved more quickly, and, well, he—"

"You don't have to speak of it, Mr. George."

He accepted her token of mercy. She must understand, having lost so many brothers. "I'll go to the battlefields. Stay on the outskirts. Keep a close eye. And you can call me Oscar."

She smiled and nodded, returning to her tea, and averting her gaze again. He thought he caught a rush of color to her cheeks. He turned back to Corncob, lest his cheeks were turning a similar shade. As he did, the skittish horse jumped at the sound of an approaching carriage, knocking Oscar's iced tea all down the front of his shirt.

"Goodness!" Felicity stepped back as Oscar attempted to brush off some of the liquid. The carriage arrival and commotion with the horse brought out Mr. Barker from the house.

"We'll have to get you cleaned up, or the bees will be after you all the way to your next stop," Felicity said.

"Yes, yes. And so long as he needs a fresh shirt, he may as well stay for dinner. Felicity, fetch him one from Franklin's wardrobe. He looks to be the same size as your brother, and Frank won't mind. And a dinner jacket, too."

Normally Oscar would have refused such an offer. The look on Felicity's face—her fetching something that belonged to her brother off to war and maybe dead—nearly pierced him. But he needed to hang on at the estate as long as he could. "Thank you, that would be very kind."

Felicity gathered the tea glasses and went back inside. He already hated being out of her presence, though he had no right to feel that way.

Mr. Barker was greeting his guests, helping an older woman out of the carriage while a man came around from the other side.

"Mr. George, meet Mr. and Mrs. Henderson. They'll be joining us for dinner. And I do believe they may be interested in your portraitures."

Oscar smiled and approached the couple as if he'd never met them.

Indeed. They would be very interested in what Oscar had to offer.

~

Felicity hung tight to Franklin's dinner jacket. Her brother's room still smelled of his shave cream.

"Miss, you don't have to give Mr. George the coat. Just lend it for the meal." Ruthy sensed her friend's hesitation, but the source was misplaced.

"It's not about the coat. In four seconds, I fell for a man who'll be dead or missing or captured by the time the next battle breaks out. Oscar said as much. He's going to the front."

"You don't know, Miss. Could be things turn out alright."

"Maybe. But by then, Daddy will have given me away to one of the railroad goons." Felicity knew good and well that she'd never allow herself to be given away, but the thought of spending an unknown number of dinners in the Barker circle of influence was nauseating.

Her stomach flopped.

She draped Franklin's clothes over her arm and strolled down the hall to the balcony doors. As much as she hated the meal, she loved seeing the carriages and wagons arrive at Little White House.

She looked over the railing. So far, the only arrivals had been the Hendersons. Oscar was at the back of the wagon with Mr. Henderson. Oscar handed him something from a wooden crate, they glanced all around, and Mr. Henderson stuck the item inside his jacket and turned toward the house.

Felicity's heart sank. Oscar was a spy. Moments ago, on her way up the steps into the house, she'd heard the introductions between Daddy and Mr. Henderson and Oscar. First-time greetings. Not catching-up greetings.

Then Oscar spotted her on the balcony, and she fumbled the clothing over the railing and fled inside.

Oscar couldn't keep his eyes off of Felicity all day, until dinner. Seated across from her, Oscar worked to engage in conversation with other guests, tried to savor the rare treat of roast and apple pie, and only dared an occasional glance in her direction when he thought she wouldn't notice.

Felicity bid her farewells to the room in a sing-song voice he'd not heard her use and feigned a long day in the heat as her reason for withdrawing. Oscar noticed outward disappointment from the two rail workers seated on either side of her father.

After Mr. Barker dismissed the table to the drawing room for glasses of precious Scotch and the servants had entered to clear the table, Oscar excused himself, saying he'd be on his way and return the clothing via post as soon as he could. Mr. Barker said he'd have none of it and insisted Oscar stay at Little White House for the night. He ordered the stable hand to board Corncob and directed him to take Franklin's room.

Because Franklin wouldn't mind. But he bet Felicity would.

Oscar's stomach knotted. He'd thanked Mr. Barker and went outside to secure Mr. Umbry's Photographic Wagon and breathe the cooling night air. He needed space between himself and the Barkers as soon as possible—and space he may get. Rumors around the table indicated a push to action along the ridge. Lookout Mountain could be the next stage of the conflict. And Oscar wanted to document it.

He climbed into the back of the small wagon, where there was barely enough room for his gear, let alone him. He prepped the supplies and crates, tethering them so he and Corncob had the best chance of making it at least part way up the ridge before any action started.

"Mr. George, going somewhere? Daddy said you'd be staying."

Oscar nearly toppled out of the wagon, but he managed to save himself and the precious supplies.

"Yes, Miss. I'm heading out tomorrow, first light."

"And in the meantime?"

He paused before he answered. A trick Mr. Umbry used often; sometimes if you wait, you may know how to better answer the hard questions.

Felicity had changed into a dark blue dress without all the hoops. She was no less stunning, even more so. A few locks of her hair had fallen loose from the rest and framed her face with soft curls which danced in the breeze. She stared a hole right through him.

When he still hadn't answered her, she said, "You're a spy, then. Yes?"

He remained silent. The questions were getting harder. He knew when the clothes toppled off the balcony that she'd seen the interaction between him and Mr. Henderson. There's no way she could know what was passed. Or who was loyal to what cause.

There's no way to know what side she was on, either. Her father was a die-hard secessionist, but that didn't make this defiant woman loyal to the South.

A tear slid down her cheek and he wanted so badly to wipe it away, but this woman could be the very death of him. If she outed him to her father, he'd be imprisoned.

"You've no idea, Mr. George, how I hate what you and my father and even dear old Mr. Umbry stand for. And Mr. Henderson and his wife scooped up an entire family as if they were a prized trinket or set of dishes. They're people, for God's sake!"

Oscar's heart flipped behind his ribs. He checked the door to the house—and the balcony—before moving in close. She was getting loud, and he feared she'd be overheard. "Felicity," he whispered low. "You've got it all wrong. About Mr. Henderson."

"But Mr. Henderson is a—"

"Unionist and trying to help that family go north. The message I passed was to help that process along. Not to bring harm." Her eyes widened, allowing more tears to spill down her cheeks. This time he used the back of his hand to wipe them away. He tucked one of those unruly curls behind her ear. "You're in great danger if you don't compose yourself."

"Ruthy." She stepped back.

"What?"

"Ruthy. Could you do the same thing for Ruthy? My servant girl."

Before he could answer—and he wanted to answer, there was no intentional pause—she blurted, "And teach me to do the same thing? Be a spy?"

He laughed and said, "Well, the first step is not to be so loud," which earned him a slap to the arm.

"I'm serious." She wiped some of her own tears away and straightened her posture.

"I believe you are very serious, Miss Felicity Barker."

"So?" This time it was she that stepped closer to him. She placed her hand gently on his forearm where she'd smacked him and rested it there. "Four seconds."

"What?"

"Four seconds for the photo to take. It was in those four seconds I knew you weren't some Railroad Roger. Knew that there was some hope to be had for a future. But not if you get killed like—"

"I have to go. I have to make some difference. All this has to stop, and I do believe Mr. Umbry was right in that the photos raise awareness and garner support. He was aligned on the wrong side of things. I have a chance to make a difference with Lookout Mountain." Concern danced across Felicity's face. "When I get back, I'll come to Little White House first. And I'll help you with Ruthy." He brushed her cheek with his knuckles, and she leaned into the caress.

"How long will you be gone?"

"Days. Weeks. Somewhere in between there my supplies will be gone." He let his hand linger on her face, then leaned in and kissed her gently on her forehead. She laid her head on his chest. Her hair had soaked up the aroma of the apple pies.

"How will you survive, Mr. George?"

"Four seconds at a time."

I Remember Paperclips

First appearing in WMG's Sweet Valentines, this bittersweet tale follows Gordon's struggle to remember the past — and to hold on to what's right in front of him…

The red runner lining the wooden floor in the upstairs hallway knew Gordon's gait quite well. The intertwining foliage and vines in the middle of the rug had faded with a million footsteps, leaving only the floral motif and red woollen background at the edges bright and unmatted—much like Gordon's memories, fading with a twinkling rim of clarity. His morning routine of orienting himself to the day ahead required much of the Persian. He and Gigi had chosen this rug from a flea market when they'd bought the house.

It used to have fringe. He remembered that.

But Sean had clipped all the glorious knots and strings away three months ago when Gordon had become stuck on his back in the upstairs hallway for half a day, cold and in pain, unable to get his feet back under him after sitting cross-legged.

Doing his counting. And sometimes his whispered chant.

Counting the strings of fringe. After he'd counted the knotted bumps in the cherry frame around the bulletin board in that same hallway. And the paperclips in his pocket.

He stuffed his hands inside his pockets, each one protecting paperclips of varying sizes. He let his fingers fill and empty of them as he paced the rug. If he concentrated, he could hear the muffled clinks they made against each other in between his socked steps. He counted steps. Five paces between Sean's room and the bathroom. Six more to his room. Eleven back again.

He counted the paperclips as they dropped from his fingertips to the bottoms of his pockets. A dozen in each.

Gordon never meant for his counting to cause others stress. It was a coping technique to keep the dementia at bay. A little obsessive, Dr. Sanders had said, but harmless. Until one becomes stuck on the hardwood floor and biology causes massive embarrassment when one's only grandson finds him in such a predicament.

That wasn't harmless to his ego.

That memory he wished the dementia would mat down like his footsteps matted the vines in the runner.

Gordon sighed and whispered, "Bend, bend, bend, slice."

He could sense something was happening today. Maybe Sean

had told him and his brain swallowed it. That happened sometimes. More frequently this month than this time last year. The swallowing of vital information. Later, after the fact and at the most inopportune moment, his mind would spit it back at him, causing him to startle. Or cry. Or wake from a deep sleep bathed in sweat and worry.

Sean was banging around in his room now, mumbling words that Gordon couldn't make out. The heavy oak door swallowed the importance of the day behind hinges and knobs. Gordon wanted to knock. But he also wanted to behave.

To be a proper adult, not in so much hourly need with incessant questions.

He didn't want to bother Sean with another inquisition. Patient as his grandson was, Sean needed his space. Gordon remembered that.

Sean was all grown up now. A big man. Gigi and Gordon had taken the boy to raise twenty years ago after that snowy day had taken their only daughter and her handsome husband. Tears again. Today was important, he knew. Tears are neither necessary nor helpful. They stressed Sean. He could see it when the boy looked at him. He wiped them on his sleeve and stuffed his hands back in his pocket.

Gordon paced in front of Sean's door, another fifteen steps back and forth, willing that instruction or date or reminder to come to the forefront on its own.

It didn't.

He rehearsed his grounding chant, unmouthed. He kept it in his head lest Sean think Dr. Sanders needed to be called today.

Bend, bend, bend, slice.

He took four paces back to the bulletin board. His right hand abandoned the paperclips and ran along the cherry frame. He and Gigi and had found the knotted and marred piece at the same flea market where they'd found the runner. Though, it used to house a mirror. Sean covered the glass with a more useful material—cork.

To help Gordon remember.

Sean tacked and paperclipped all manner of things to the board. Gordon promised to take a break several times a morning from counting steps to stand and read the board. The day of the week was pinned to the top of the board. Sean changed it every morning before Gordon got out of bed.

Today was Saturday.

Another sheet held reminders that Gordon didn't need yet, but might one day. These were printed in big block letters on a single sheet of white paper. Black and bold in bossy capitals, those commands. Shower. Bathe. Teeth. Those sorts of things.

Other reminders like doctor appointments or haircuts were scribbled in Sean's handwriting and tacked next to the daily to-do list.

Two cards hung on the bulletin board this morning.

One was for Dr. Sanders later next week. A kind lady sometimes, but bossy like the capital letters at others. She'd helped him with his dementia meds and mental exercises to try to keep those bright specks around the edges from fading away.

Sean continued to thud and stomp and mumble behind his bedroom door. Gordon ignored the ruckus and pulled the other card from its pin. He ran his fingers along two sentences, printed one on top of the other. Blue ink. Sean's writing. The first line said: *Today is Valentine's Day.*

A flicker started in the deep recesses of Gordon's mind. Valentine's day.

The day he and Gigi had gone to Sean's second-grade class party. The school had invited the parents to serve snacks and share interesting tales about their work and life. Bring a treat or keepsake.

And little Sean, blond curls and green eyes, didn't want Pops and Gigi to come. Said their work was boring and all the other kids had *real* parents coming.

Gordon had wanted to paddle the boy, or at the very least take away his playtime or dessert. Teach him how to show respect. Gigi had other thoughts. "Tell them about your paperclips. How they're made. About how they bind things together like love binds us." Gigi reached for her necklace where a paperclip shaped into a rough circle the size of her left ring finger had hung for nearly thirty years.

"And what will you do to impress our young charge?" Gordon remembered the days even further back when he'd feared he'd never be able to impress the love of his life. He hadn't even been able to afford a proper wedding band. Silver steel had to do. Gigi had been so patient as he'd fumbled from his knees to unbend the paperclip and work the thin metal around and around her small finger.

She'd said yes, and he'd promised once the factory reinstated the overtime that he'd get her a proper ring. She'd worn the handmade one around her neck until her last day.

Gigi grinned at him. Sparkle in her eyes. "Why, Gordon, dear. I'll do what I do best."

And she did. She'd whipped out her sewing basket and created tiny hearts stuffed with dabs of white cotton fluff. She sewed the tops together with a loop of ribbon. Pinks and reds and whites and a few blues for the too-tough boys, including Sean. She embroidered each child's name onto a heart.

Gordon drew a makeshift diagram of his station at the paperclip machine on the blackboard. He remembered how the white dust clung to his fingertips as he drug the chalk across the slate. He showed the knobs where the thin steel would bend, bend, bend the metal. He drew the blade that would slice the paperclip from the spool. He mimicked the sounds the machine made as he explained the process, and by the end of his talk, the kids chanted to each other and marched and hopped to the rhythm of "Bend, Bend, Bend, Slice."

Afterward, the class used the stash of paperclips in Gordon's pockets to hang each of their hearts above the blackboard in that little second-grade classroom.

The kids had cheered.

Sean apologized later and never complained, at least not to Pops or Gigi, that fate and tragedy had left a couple of old geezers to look after him.

Tears again. His sleeve would be soaked before Sean emerged from his room, but Gordon was pleased this memory stayed with him, sparkling and clear.

Today is Valentine's Day.

Under that line, Sean had written: *Today I propose to Miriam.*

That was it! Sean's big day. Gordon replaced the card on the bulletin board and stuffed his hands back in his pockets just as Sean stumbled into the hallway, pulling on his trouser socks. "Pops, you doin' okay out here?"

"Morning, Sean."

Sean's shoulders drooped a little and Sean patted Gordon on the shoulder. That meant Gordon had done or said something wrong. Or had forgotten something. Again. "The nurse will be here soon."

Nurse. Gordon wasn't much on the nurse, but after the incident in this hallway, Sean insisted someone be in the house with him if Sean were to be gone more than an hour. And today was Sean's big day. Gordon had forgotten, though he knew now that Sean had talked about this for days. Maybe weeks.

It was hard to remember.

"You remember what today is, Pops?"

Gordon grinned. Happy that he'd taken the time to study the corkboard. "I sure do. You got the ring?"

"Got the ring in my pocket. Got the roses downstairs." Sean fiddled with his bowtie.

"Awful early for formal wear." Gordon paused, confusion threatening to destroy the moment. "Have we had breakfast yet?"

"Bacon, Pops. And soup for lunch, and the nurse will heat your dinner up." He wrestled the black silk around his collar and tried to tie the piece. "I've got a photographer hiding to capture her reaction, so you can see. She'll be all dolled up, too. I'm about to sweat all the way through my jacket." He made a sour face and whipped the tie from the collar.

"You got the ring?" It had to be better than what Gordon had proposed to his Gigi with. Sean had a good job, though Gordon couldn't remember Sean's title right off hand... A tick of panic set in his chest. He wanted to remember this moment. His grandson all grown up and off to start a new adventure.

Bend, bend, bend, slice.

Sean took Gordon's shoulder again. "I got the ring, Pops. What I don't got is how this dumb bowtie works." Sean tried to smooth the fabric against his pants. Gordon took it from him and turned his grandson toward the wall, facing the bulletin board.

Gordon upturned the stiff white collar and laid the black silk in proper position. He fumbled at first, not having done this particular task for eons. Sean helped a little, old and young hands struggling to work the fabric into a bow worthy of an important event. They managed to get it tied, but it was still just slightly crooked. "I just wanted today to be perfect, Pops."

"I remember my day with Gigi. It wasn't perfect, but she said yes anyway."

Sean faced Gordon and tugged at the bow, trying to get it straight. Above his head the corkboard reminded Gordon that today was Saturday.

Valentine's Day. Sean's big day.

"Do you have the ring?"

Sean stopped fussing with the tie and reached into his pocket. He pulled out a simple circle of thin gauged steel.

"That's your Gigi's." Gordon took it from Sean's palm.

"That's still okay, right Pops? We talked about this."

Gordon let his tears chase down his cheeks right down to the stubble on his chin. "Yes, Sean. It's perfect." He handed the ring back to Sean. "Gigi would be proud. Your mom and dad, too."

"I'm glad you remember her, Pops. All of them. I'm glad you remember them." Sean's eyes brimmed wet and he replaced the ring into jacket pocket then reached again for that crooked bowtie.

Gordon retrieved one of the twelve paperclips from his right pocket and began unwinding it, shaping the ends into tiny loops. He threaded the wire behind the tie and worked the black silk and the white collar into submission. "I don't remember breakfast."

"Bacon." Sean reached to feel the tie. "Hey, it's straight. Great job, Pops!"

Pride welled up in Gordon, an all-too-strange feeling these days. Pride for Sean. Pride that he'd done something important to help, though he couldn't quite grasp what that was...

Bend, bend, bend, slice.

The pair headed for the top of the steps. "Sean?"

"Yeah, Pops?"

Gordon grinned. "I *do* remember paperclips."

About the Author

Beth enjoys chucking words into sentences then standing back to see what magic—or mayhem—falls out, crafting tales in mystery, sci-fi, fantasy, and general "slice of life" fiction. She couldn't accomplish this without the help of her tutu-clad Little Miss Muse and Trudi the Concrete Office Goose, who's partial to superhero capes.

Her stories have appeared in multiple publications, including Pulphouse Fiction Magazine and Ellery Queen Mystery Magazine, and in multiple fiction anthologies. She's received several Honorable Mentions from Writers of the Future. Her lighthearted blog peeks into the writing life as she pokes fun at herself and her circus of a life.

Follow the antics of Little Miss Muse and Trudi, read Beth's blog (she might have burned down her kitchen last week), and discover the stories at bapaul.com.